MARRYING THE MONSTERS: A HISTORICAL MONSTER EROTICA COLLECTION

Lilith Leana

Table of Contents

Acknowledgement

A big thank you to my husband for always believing in me and never making me feel like I couldn't do it.

Cover art

Cover art photo from Depositphoto

Cover design

Lilith Leana with Canva

Brief Summary

Marrying the Orc

Violet's father arranges a marriage for her, but she wants to be free of society's expectations of her. She runs to her Orc stable hand, asking him to make her his.

Grant has loved Violet since he was young. When she offers herself to him, he cannot refuse, but he will do the right thing to marry her before he makes her his.

Will she regret losing her family name by marrying for freedom, or will they live happily ever after?

Marrying the Minotaur

Lilly needs a husband to ensure the bloodline and the inheritance of her father's estate. When she meets a new Minotaur Earl at the last ball of the season, he seems like the perfect candidate.

Ian, bored with his new title and duties to the crown, accepts a deal from a delectable woman he cannot refuse, but on one condition: he will have her in his bed at every possible opportunity.

Will their marriage become real in every possible way, or will Lilly regret marrying a beast?

Marrying the Gargoyle

Daisy almost loses her life but gets saved by a handsome Gargoyle. He needs a companion, and she requires a husband. They make a deal for a marriage in name only, but Daisy wants more of him.

Jacob has been happy with his long but lonely life until Daisy comes in and disrupts everything with her soft touches and whispered promises.

Will she be able to break his stony exterior, or will she be alone in her marriage?

READER ADVISORY: THIS story contains explicit sex scenes between a human and a Monster. Marrying the Monsters is a collection of the three previously published short stories featuring the Bennet sisters and their monster husbands with an added Epilogue.

Marrying the Monsters is a 25k words, steamy, hot, erotic, Regency, short story collection. Explicit sex scenes, standalone, no cheating or cliffhangers.

Marrying the Orc
The Proposal

"**I** will not marry him!"

My voice thundered through the room, and my father looked at me with lifted eyebrows. Never in my life had I raised my voice to him. I was always a dutiful daughter and proudly represented the Bennet family name as the eldest, but I would not let him pawn me off as if I were some kind of possession that could be changed hands by the will of men.

"Yes, you will, Violet," my father said, turning away from me. "I have already made the arrangements. You are to marry him in a fortnight."

I took a step back as if he had slapped me. A rushed wedding was an even bigger insult. Society would think we had something to hide, or that I was already with child.

"Why?" I asked when he looked at me again.

That one word hung between us, getting heavier with each passing second. My father averted his gaze again and sighed.

"For once, you will do as you are told, Violet."

I shook my head, unable to believe my father was capable of such cruelty. Marrying me off as if I were some cheap whore to a man twice my age and with more dead wives than I had sisters. I realized there was no use in arguing with him and turned to leave the room with calm strides, even though my insides were whirling around like a storm.

As soon as I closed the door, I picked up my skirts and ran outside to the one place where I felt safe, the stables. My best friend, Grant, the Orc that handled our horses, was waiting for me. He turned around and immediately opened his arms when he saw me running towards him.

The moment his massive, muscular green arms surrounded me, I felt like I could breathe again. Grant has been my safe haven ever since he arrived at our land. He had been just a boy looking for a home, and I was a young girl desperate to break free from the confinements of my title as the eldest of the Bennet family.

"What is it, Violet? Speak to me and share your sorrows," Grant said as he caressed my hair in soothing movements.

I relaxed against his massive frame as I told him everything that had happened. He sat down on a hay bale, keeping me close to him. When the words marriage came out of my mouth, his body tensed, but he kept caressing me, calming me, and giving me the courage to finish my story.

"But I cannot marry him, Grant," I said as I looked up. "Because I wish to marry you."

He arched his eyebrows up as he looked down at me. Even seated, he towered high above me. He was so tall that he could control every horse without even breaking a sweat. I had watched him many times, feeling a fluttering in my stomach every time he flexed those bulging muscles. I knew that marrying him would fill my life with happiness, a stark contrast to the fear I felt towards marrying our neighboring Lord.

"Me?" Grant asked.

"Yes, you, Grant. My best friend, my confidant, the Orc I cannot imagine a life without," I said as I grabbed his hand and put it against my lips. I kissed his fingers one by one. "The Orc that has visited my dreams many nights."

His breathing stuttered as he watched me slowly suck on his thumb. "Violet," he whispered, his voice rough with need.

I could feel his heart beat strong inside of his chest, and I longed for it to belong to me, as mine belonged to him.

"Please Grant," I said, my voice trembling with trepidation, "tell me you love me too."

I couldn't bring myself to meet his gaze, afraid of the rejection that might be reflected in his eyes. Playing with his massive fingers, I loved how free I could be with my touches for the first time, hoping he would feel the same. I had dreamed of this moment countless times, never imagining I would have the courage to express my feelings to him. Yet, the actions of my father had driven me here to seek solace in his embrace.

"Of course I do, but I am but a lowly stable hand. I could never give you the life you deserve," Grant said.

His confession made my heart flutter in my chest. As I looked up, I could see his words reflected in his gorgeous brown eyes, and I knew we would be happy together.

"Would you treat me with love, respect, and devotion?" I asked.

"Of course, but Violet-"

"That is all I want from you. Please Grant. Take me, ruin me, make me yours," I said as I jumped up to grab his neck.

On instinct, he put his arms around me. I grabbed his soft hair and pulled his mouth down on mine. He didn't resist and in moments, our lips met in my first kiss. It was everything I had imagined and yet, so much more because it was with Grant, the Orc I loved since the first time he helped me after I fell off a horse. His tusks grazed my cheeks and his lips were soft underneath mine. He tasted like a summer's night and freedom.

He broke off the kiss far too soon, panting as if he had just tamed a horse. I wanted so much more than one kiss from him, and I already leaned in for another, but he held me back.

"Violet, I cannot... we must not... it is not proper..."

"Would you rather me marry an old man who holds me in no higher regard than a horse in his stable?" I asked, pushing out my lower lip and tilting my chin up.

"Never," Grant growled as his grip tightened on me and arousal coursed through me.

His stunning brown eyes burned with lust, and I could see that he did everything to contain his feelings for me. I did not want him to restrain or hold back his emotions. My desire was for them to burst free, like a dam breaking and flooding the surrounding fields.

"Please, Grant. My heart already belongs to you. Take my body as well."

I could feel his massive body tremble against mine, still trying so hard to contain his feelings. I lifted my chin higher, begging him to kiss me again with my eyes.

"I will marry you. But I will do it the proper way. Please, Violet, pick out a dress, pack a bag, and tell your sisters. I will arrange for us to marry in the Chapel this evening and I will have you in my bed right after," Grant said, caressing my cheek with one of his big fingers.

My heart almost jumped out of my chest from joy, and my lips curved into a smile. We would finally be together, as I had imagined so many times before.

"Kiss me again, so I have your taste on my lips as I leave you to get ready," I said.

"I could never deny you anything, my little flower," Grant said as he bent his head down to kiss me again.

I moaned against his lips, climbing on his lap to get closer to him. His hands circled my hips, almost encompassing them entirely. I opened my mouth to let my tongue out to play, licking his lips to coax his tongue out. He groaned, granting me access to his mouth. Our tongues touched each other, and excitement and arousal coursed through me.

I could hardly wait for our marriage to start so I could have him on our wedding night. There were so many things I wanted to do to him. I wanted to touch him, taste him, feel him inside of me. My hands yearned to explore every inch of his bare flesh. Grant broke off the kiss before I could let it go any further.

"Go Violet, before I forget what is proper, and take you here in the stables like an animal."

I moaned, not at all opposed to that proposition, but he sat me down on my feet, caressing my cheek with a gentle touch to soften his rejection.

"Go Violet, we will be husband and wife soon enough and I will show you all the pleasures our union will have to offer."

"I love you," I said

"And I you, my little flower."

The Wedding

I ran to my sisters, my heart light and my smile as big as it could fit on my face. I would be free, together with Grant. The only heaviness I felt in my heart was because I had to leave my dear sisters behind. We only had each other since our mother died, relying on each other for comfort and compassion. Ever since her death, my father has become a completely different person, disappearing from our house for days at a time without a word.

I stormed into the drawing room where my sisters were busy with needling and reading. Daisy looked up from her book while Lilly cursed as she pricked her finger.

"Sisters, I am to be married," I said breathlessly, still not entirely believing it was going to happen.

"What, to whom?" my youngest sister, Daisy, asked as he put her book down.

"Grant," I said, twirling around the room.

"Father approved?" Lilly asked, forgetting about her needlework.

At the mention of our father, my smile fell, and I shook my head. "No, he wanted me to marry Lord Canbry."

"That old man?" Daisy asked with a scrunched-up nose.

"That is why I have to leave to marry Grant. I cannot stay here and marry that beast of a man."

"His fourth wife only died last year. Should he not still be in mourning?" Daisy asked, disdain lacing her voice.

"It does not matter," Lilly said with a laugh, grabbing my hands and twirling around with me. "She is to marry Grant. How joyous news, sister. How can we help?"

"I need a dress, some clothes for on the road and my pin money. I am certain Father will not be pleased, so I should forget about my Dowry."

Daisy sighed and got up to join us. "I do not approve, sister, but if it is what makes you happy, I shall refrain from saying so."

"He makes me happy, Daisy."

She nodded with a serious look on her face. Daisy was the most studious of us three always with her head in a book. She was still too young to have the threat of a marriage hanging above her, but wise for her years.

"You can wear Mother's dress. And we shall both give you our pin money as well. You will need it, marrying a stable hand," Daisy said.

"Oh, of course. We have no need for pin money this year since neither of us is out in society yet and we have plenty of dresses," Lilly said.

They both left the room to gather what was needed while I went to gather mine. I did not pack much, some undergarments and a few light summer dresses. Everything I had was far too flamboyant and impractical for my new life with Grant. Nerves and butterflies flew around in my stomach, realizing I would leave everything I knew behind.

My sisters returned carrying our mother's wedding dress. It was out of fashion, but beautiful and it fit me like a glove. The dress had sleeves crafted from a stunning, delicate lace and the skirt moved with the grace of air. Looking at myself in the mirror wearing the soft white dress, surrounded by my sisters, made me miss her so much.

"You look beautiful," Lilly said.

"She would have been proud of you," Daisy said. "Our happiness was always the most important thing to her."

"I miss her," I said and my sisters agreed, hugging me.

"Now go, before Father comes back and drags you to Lord Canbry," Daisy said, discretely wiping away a tear.

"Thank you both," I said as I accepted their pin money, joining it with mine in a small satchel. "I will write letters and maybe when we have a boy, Father will accept him and we can return to the Estate."

"We will look forward to your letters, sister," Lilly said. "Now go, marry Grant, and love with all of your heart."

"I will," I said and after a last hug, I left my family home to meet my soon-to-be-husband.

Grant had prepared my horse for me, and my heart felt warm as I saw her saddled and ready in the stable. Light as a feather, I rode to the Chapel where my Orc was waiting for me. With only the priest as our witness, we married in the dead of night, starting our life together.

The Wedding Night

My heart felt so light that I might fly away with it. I was finally free. Free of my father, free of the rules of society, and free to love who I wanted. Grant's hand in mine felt warm and secure, and I couldn't wait for our marriage to be consummated. I heard so many different tales, but I knew it would feel right with him.

In what felt like mere moments, we were at the Inn where he had reserved a room for us. When the Innkeeper saw me in my wedding dress and the smiles on our faces, he upgraded us to the master suit for the night. Happiness radiated through me. Tonight was all ours. I knew we would need to face the consequences of our actions tomorrow and think up a plan on how we would survive, but that mattered not at this moment.

We fell into the room laughing, our hands never straying far away from one another. I craved his touch and did not want to wait another moment to experience it.

"I have waited to feel your soft skin underneath my hands for so long, Violet," Grant groaned.

"Yes, naked, now," I moaned as I pulled at his shirt.

We tore off each other clothes, not caring what ripped and what remained whole. I needed him more than I needed my next breath, and it appeared that he felt the same. The moment I freed his massive cock from its confinement, I wrapped my fingers around him, earning a strangled groan from my husband. My fingers didn't even meet, as his girth was far too impressive. His cock was a darker green than his skin, so much darker than my pale fingers surrounding it. Throbbing veins covered his length, making me want to explore every single one of them.

"Wait, Violet," Grant groaned. "Or I will spend in your hands."

"I am certain you can spend more than once in an evening," I said, more confident than I really was.

All my knowledge of the marital bed had come from whispers between maids, and none of them had been with an Orc. His massive cock fascinated me and I didn't want to let him go until I had pleasured him to completion, as was my marital duty as his wife.

"Please, Violet. Your hand feels too good."

"Let me make you feel wonderful, my husband," I said as I moved my hand up and down.

Grant groaned low as his hand covered mine, squeezing much firmer than I had done and moving much faster. His face contorted in pleasure as our hands caressed his cock together. The muscles in his arm and stomach flexed as my arousal rose. It was an addictive feeling to give my husband pleasure and to see it on his face.

I watched, fascinated, as his hands kept a punishing pace, imagining him thrusting inside of me in the same way. The sounds that came from him only fueled my own desire, as I could feel his cock throb underneath my hand. I wondered how long it would take when his passionate grunts became louder.

I gasped as I could feel his seed travel through his cock and after a few caresses, his body trembled and his release spurted out. Grant came an unearthly amount. Spurt after spurt of his cum shot out of his cock, covering our hands and his stomach in his seed as he stifled his hungry growl.

I could not resist the urge to dip my finger in the cum and taste it. His earthy, rich taste exploded in my mouth and I moaned as I could feel arousal course through me. I could not wait to do that again, and again, and perhaps even use my mouth next time.

"My world, Violet. That was..."

With his clean hand, he cupped my cheek, caressing it with his thumb in a move so intimate I could feel it deep in my soul.

"Did it feel good?" I asked breathlessly.

"Amazing. Let me make you feel this good, too. Please, I need to taste my wife," Grant said.

"Yes, please," I moaned.

Grant turned us around until I lay on the bed on my back, my legs spread wide and my husband in between them. I had no idea what to expect, but as soon as his tongue touched my pussy, pleasure sparked inside of me. His tongue was a deep shade of pink, in stark contrast with his green skin and pale tusks.

"I want to taste every inch of you, but I will devour your pussy first," Grant growled.

"Yes, Grant," I purred.

His tongue did things to me I could have never imagined. Pleasure flowed through me as his massive tongue licked me within an inch of my life. I didn't know what to do with my hands, my legs, or my thoughts. It felt like too much, but also not enough. As if sensing that I needed more than his tongue, he pushed one meaty finger inside of me.

I've always loved Grant's green hands, massive and gentle at the same time. And now that I had one of his fingers inside of me, I wanted more.

"More," I begged, my voice hoarse with pleasure as I opened my legs wider, pushing my hips up.

"Such a greedy wife," Grant growled against my pussy as he gave me what I craved.

He entered another finger, fucking me slowly with them until I was used to the intrusion. His tongue flicked over my pleasure bud as his fingers pleasured me from the inside. The sensation of his tusks grazing the inside of my thighs made waves of pleasure course through me, but I ached for more, fully aware of the size difference between his fingers and his cock.

"More," I moaned, and he grumbled in response.

My breathing was shallow, and I could feel the pleasure rise inside of me. His tongue and fingers did things to me that were beyond my wildest imagination. The sounds he made while tasting me made me feel like I was the most delicious meal of his life. When I could easily take two of his fingers, he added a third one. A low throaty sound of pleasure escaped me when he stretched me and pleasure filled me.

"Yes, please, Grant," I sighed as my pussy squeezed around his fingers.

Grant thrust his fingers inside of me as he flicked his tongue over my pleasure bud again and again. Pleasure rose inside of me, becoming bigger than I could have ever imagined.

Everything became too overwhelming, and at that moment, I fractured into a million pieces. A pleasured cry tore from my throat as my pussy clenched around his fingers. He groaned and kept licking me as pleasure washed over me. My whole body trembled and my legs spasmed as pleasure took over my senses. The feeling was so foreign, but addictive at the same time. I already knew I wanted to experience it again and again with my husband.

With gentle licks, Grant let me come down from my high as he pulled out his fingers. The most obscene sounds came from my wet pussy as he dragged them out. He groaned and licked off the wetness from his fingers as his eyes connected with mine. I was panting, and a blush spread over my body, but my cheeks heated up even more when I saw him lick his fingers one by one.

"Delicious," Grant groaned. "I'll have you for breakfast for the rest of our lives, my wife."

"I am hoping for nothing less, my husband," I said as I stretched out my arms and arched my back, pushing my breasts up. "If this is what married life is like, we should have married years ago."

His eyes turned dark with lust as he crawled on top of me. "Then we must make up for years lost," Grant said and kissed me.

I moaned into his mouth, loving the way his taste mixed with mine. His cock was hard again, poking against my stomach, and I was achingly empty, ready to be filled by my Orc husband.

I wrapped my legs around his hips, pressing my wet pussy against his cock. He groaned against my lips, breaking the kiss to look between us. With one hand, he grabbed his cock and slowly guided himself inside. He was still so much bigger than his three fingers, but my wetness and his seed eased the way. His big cock head slid inside, and I moaned when he stretched my pussy to fit.

"How do you feel, my love?" Grant asked as he paused, breathing heavily.

"So full, but I need more," I moaned as I pulled him in deeper with my legs.

Grant made a hoarse sound of pleasure as he gave me several more inches, stretching my pussy in the most delicious way. He pulled out slightly, pushing back inside, giving me even more of him, but I wanted it all.

"More, Grant, more," I begged.

"Easy Violet. I do not wish to hurt you."

"You will hurt my feelings if you do not fuck me properly, my husband," I said.

Grant growled low, eyes closed as he sunk in the rest of the way until his hips were flush with mine, leaving no space between our bodies. I felt a rush of air leave my lungs as his cock speared me like a spit roast. I've never felt so full or so complete in my life.

"Fuck, Violet, you feel so tight around my cock," Grant groaned.

"So big," I moaned. "Now fuck me, husband."

Grant slowly pulled back and thrust inside of me again, sparking pleasure, mixed with a tinge of pain. He repeated the motion again and again and after the third thrust, only pleasure remained. It felt even better than having his tongue on me. I could feel every breath he took and the strong beat of his heart as our bodies connected in the most intimate of ways.

"Mine," Grant growled as he fucked me with full earnestness.

I moaned in response, unable to utter a single tangible word as he fucked me as if his life depended on it. His massive body crowded me and his chest rubbed my breasts with each thrust, but I didn't feel suffocated. I felt safe underneath him, knowing he would never do anything to harm me.

His cock touched every pleasure point inside of me, sparking desire with each thrust. I could already feel my pleasure growing inside of me, ready to burst. If I had known making love could feel like this, I would have done it so much sooner with him.

Sounds came from me I've never made before, all filled with pleasure and desire for this Orc that was truly making me his. His feral sounds of pleasure filled my ears, and I knew I would remember them for many years to come. The grunts, groans, and moans sounded brutish and ferocious, but seeing them reflected on his face, I knew they were made out of all-consuming pleasure.

"My wife," Grant growled.

His dazzling brown eyes burned bright with passion as he fucked me even harder. My hands were all over him, touching every inch of green skin I could find. I knew we had our whole lives ahead of us, but I wanted to memorize all of him, every intake of his breath, every thrust of his cock.

"My husband," I moaned as my pussy squeezed around his cock.

His thrusts faltered as my pussy seemed to take on a life of its own. My climax was so close that I could almost taste it on my tongue. After a few more thrusts, it finally burst, and I screamed with my release. Pleasure washed over me as my pussy gripped his cock tight. Grant groaned as if in pain, but before I could ask him, he erupted inside of me. His cock throbbed as my pussy milked it of its seed and the sounds of our pleasure filled the room.

My whole body trembled and my legs quivered as my pussy took all of his seed. It was so much that I could feel it flowing out of me, ruining the bedsheets. Pleasure took over all my senses, and I didn't even care about the mess we made.

I could feel his body tremble as he supported his weight on his broad arms. With a gentle kiss, he pulled out, making even more cum flow from my pussy. Grant groaned when he saw the mess we made. Kneeling between my legs, he studied my pussy. He scooped up some cum and pushed back inside of me. I moaned when his finger entered my abused pussy, but it felt too good to tell him to stop.

"So beautiful covered in my seed," Grant growled as he pushed in more of his cum.

"Why are you doing that?" I asked, as my pussy squeezed around his finger.

"It feels natural to me," Grant mumbled. His head shot up and his eyes focused on me. "How does it feel to you?"

"So good," I moaned. "When can you fuck me again?"

His laugh rumbled through me as he gave me more of his cum. "I think I promised to taste every inch of you. And I would not want our marriage to start off with a lie."

I stretched my arms up and pushed my breasts high. "We would not want that, my dear husband. Every inch of my body is yours to do with as you please."

"It would be my pleasure to taste you," Grant said as he lifted my foot up to his mouth.

A giggle escaped me as his lips and tusks grazed the bottom of my foot. "Are you ticklish, my wife?" Grant asked.

He picked up my other foot and repeated the motion, earning him another laugh of me. "Maybe a little. Please do go about tasting more of me."

Grant angled my foot so he could kiss my ankle, calf, shin, and up to my knee. It felt like a slow seduction after our passionate lovemaking, and I loved every second of it. He gave both my legs the same treatment until he reached the junction where I was still wet with our combined release. His tusks grazed the insides of my thighs and a shiver of delight washed over me. He flicked out his tongue to taste me again, making him growl low.

"You are delicious," Grant groaned.

"But there is still so much more to taste of me," I said, pushing my breasts up.

My nipples were hard and aching for his touch. I may have been a virgin at the start of this evening, but I knew where my body ached for him.

"I married a wise woman," Grant said as he leaned over me.

His mouth descended on my breasts and I moaned at the first contact. His hot lips trailed over the valley of my breasts, kissing every inch of them as his tusks skimmed over my sensitive skin. When he was satisfied he had kissed everywhere, his tongue came out to play. His hot, wet tongue flicked over my nipple and I gasped as pleasure bubbled up inside of me.

"Delicious, like the sweetest fruit," Grant said as he licked my other nipple.

"Yes, Grant, more," I moaned as I grabbed his soft hair to keep him close to my breasts.

It was an amazing feeling, yet so different from his mouth on my pussy. Together with him, I discovered the many facets pleasure had to offer and how much more we would learn from each other bodies. When my fingers grazed behind his ear, I could feel his entire body tremble on top of me, so I repeated the motion again and again until he sighed with pleasure.

"How does that feel so good?" Grant asked.

"I do not know, but I want to discover more of you as well, my husband," I said as I let my hands wander over his neck and shoulders.

"I will never tire of hearing you say that, my wife."

"That I wish to please you as well, or that you are my husband?"

"Both. All of it. Every word out of your mouth is like a caress on my ugly skin," Grant said with his eyes closed.

"You are not ugly," I said as I pulled his face up to mine.

He was an Orc, and his features were not as elegant as those of a Gargoyle or a human, but there was so much beauty in his being.

"I love the color of your eyes, as it reminds me of the sweetest chocolate. I love the color of your skin as it resembles the first leaves coming in spring. I love your mouth and tusks," I said as I let my hands wander over his features. "Because they may look frightening, but I know what pleasure that mouth is capable of."

"Truly?" Grant asked, opening his eyes slowly to look at my face as if to expect disgust.

"Yes. And we have our whole lives ahead of us for me to let you know how much I love every part of you. I married you, Grant. Not because I needed to get away, but because I love you. I think I have loved you from the first moment you helped me on my horse." I grabbed his hand and lifted it up to my lip, kissing every finger. "Your hands were massive, but gentle as you helped me and my horse understand each other."

"I have loved you from the first time you screamed at me when you thought I had startled the horses. Such a small girl, barely coming up to my shoulder, but fierce and beautiful. Never fearful of me. My brave little flower."

His words were like a fire inside of me, igniting a burning inferno of need.

"I think you should show me how much you love me again," I panted as I grabbed his hardening cock.

With a few caresses, he was rock hard again, and in moments he was inside of me. We both groaned as he filled me up with his massive cock. My pussy was still sensitive, and Grant moved his hips in a slow, seductive rhythm as if we had all the time in the world to chase our high.

Our eyes never left each other, and I could see every emotion and spark of pleasure on his face. He might think he was ugly, but he was beautiful to me. My Orc, my husband, my Grant.

The Honeymoon

I woke up to the rumbling of my stomach, realizing I had not eaten since supper and had done much more strenuous activities than I was used to. Grant's arm lay across my belly and I could feel his cock poke me from behind. When I moved, he rumbled and pulled me closer to him.

With a laugh, I tried to entangle myself, but he would not let me go. "Why would my wife want to leave our marital bed so soon already?" Grant grumbled.

"Because your wife is hungry," I said, my words emphasized by the rumbling of my stomach again.

"I will feed you," Grant said and kissed my cheek, pulling himself up.

As he got up from the bed, I could see his muscles flex in the sunlight. I looked at his magnificent body, still not believing he was truly mine. Grant caught my gaze and his eyes burned bright with passion.

"If you continue looking at me like that, I will feed you my cock for breakfast."

I gasped, realizing I was not at all opposed to the suggestion. Grant laughed as he saw my face light up. He pulled on his shirt and pants and gave me a gentle kiss.

"Maybe later. First, I need to make sure you have a full belly so you have energy for the day to come."

"Thank you, my husband."

The day had come far too quickly for my liking. We needed to figure out a place to live and find jobs. What could I do that would be of any use? All I had learned was how to be a good wife to a Lord and how to run a household, both of which would not be useful married to a stable hand. I waited until regret would cloud my mind, but it didn't. Whatever we would face, we would face together, and having Grant by my side was the best thing that could have happened to me.

I pulled the sheet around me as I brushed my hair. It was an absolute mess from our nightly activities. Grant had grabbed my hair on multiple occasions and I could feel my cheeks heat up from the memories. How was it possible that I never knew what pleasure could exist at the hands of a monster? I should inform my sisters about them, so they can prepare for their wedding night.

Grant returned with a steaming bowl of porridge that I gratefully accepted. It wasn't as delicious as I was used to, but it filled my belly and it was our first meal together as newlyweds. Anything he would have given me would have been perfect.

"The warden asked if we were to stay another night or would vacate the room," Grant said.

"How much is another night? How much do we have?" I asked.

Grant pulled out his pouch and laid the contents on the table. "We might be able to stay another night, but we will need to look for work tomorrow."

"Oh wait," I said as I grabbed my own pouch. "I forgot to add mine."

I had gathered all my pin money and had received my sisters as well, representing a miserable dowry, but hopefully enough for now. I laid the content on the table next to Grants and his eyes widened.

"Will this help?" I asked.

"Violet. Do you have any idea how much money this is?" Grant asked.

"Not as much as my dowry, I imagine, but would you think it enough to marry me? How long could we live off this?" I asked.

I knew how much silk or lace I could buy with it, but I had no idea of the cost of living. My father handled all the finances of our household and I never thought to ask.

"I did not marry you for your money, Violet, but this will be enough to support us for a year, depending on how frugal we live."

"Truly?" I asked.

My pin money was scarcely enough for dresses to last me a season, but I had no need for such frivolousness anymore.

Grant nodded as he put some coins in a pile on the side. "This is enough to rent a small cabin." He created two more piles and added. "This will be enough for food and this for our starting necessities, like clothes for you. It depends on what you find important in life."

Even with those three piles, there was still plenty left. "All I need is you, Grant. I do not care for pretty dresses or jewelry. As long as I have you by my side, I can be dressed in rags and be happy."

"I love you, Violet. But this will make the start of our life much easier and give us time to find work."

"And gives us time to enjoy our honeymoon?" I asked as I crawled on his lap.

Grant pulled the sheet away, exposing my naked body to his heated gaze.

"So much time to enjoy our honeymoon," he growled as his lips descended on mine.

Our tongues met in a passionate dance and I could feel arousal course through me. I craved his cock inside of me again. My hands fumbled with his pants, but he helped me open them. He groaned when I closed my hand around his hardening cock. I loved how eager he was for me as well. Within moments, his cock was hard and at my entrance. I gasped as he entered me, stretching my pussy to take all of his cock.

"Fuck, Violet, so wet and ready for me," Grant growled as he pushed his hips up.

"Yes. I need your cock," I moaned as my pussy clenched around him.

"It is all yours," Grant groaned as his hands grabbed my hips and he helped me bounce on his cock.

Pleasure rose inside of me with each thrust of his cock. My hands gripped his shoulders to keep me steady as moans tumbled from my lips.

"My beautiful, gorgeous wife," Grant said.

Pleasure contorted his face, and his tusks jutted forward as he bit his lip. I had never seen a more beautiful sight before. How could he think of himself as ugly when all I could see was my amazing husband, whom I wanted to spend the rest of my life with?

"Grant, Yes. Grant, Please," I moaned, unable to voice my feelings consumed by the pleasure he was giving me.

Grant growled low, increasing the speed of his thrusts. One of his hands went in between my legs, locating my pleasure bud. He circled the little bud and my pussy squeezed around his cock, sparking pleasure deep inside of me.

Sounds of pleasure fell from my lips as his cock and finger did everything in their power to please me.

"Are you going to come around my cock?" Grant asked.

I nodded as my pussy pulsed around his cock, so close to bursting that I had no words to use. He fucked me harder as the pressure on my pleasure bud increased. I was experiencing too much at the same time and before I could voice it; I burst into a million pieces. Pleasure washed over me as my pussy clenched around his cock.

"Yes, Violet. Come for me, squeeze my cock," Grant growled.

After a few more thrusts, I could feel his cock throb deep inside of me, filling me with his seed. His whole body trembled as his face contorted with pleasure. My own pleasure only increased by seeing his consume him. I loved every twitch of his eye, and the quiver of his lip as his cock throbbed inside of me, sharing his release with me.

After we caught our breath and cleaned up, we decided to search for our new home. We had little to pack, so in mere moments, we were on our way to start our lives as a married couple. Luck was on our side and in only a few hours we had the key to a small cabin on the edge of the woods rented to us by a lovely elderly couple of Trolls. It did help that we were able to pay the first six months' rent in advance without making a big dent in our finances.

As soon as we arrived at the cabin, Grant swung me up in his arms, making me giggle.

"What are you doing?"

"Carrying my wife over the threshold of our home," Grant said.

"Our home," I said with a smile. "I like the sound of that."

"Me too."

As he stepped into the little cabin, I looked around. It was small but had high enough ceilings so Grant would not hit his head. Dust covered the furniture, but it all looked sturdy enough. It was a far cry from the manor I was used to, but I had everything I needed right here with me.

Grant let out an annoyed huff as he looked around.

"What is it?" I asked.

"I wanted to lay you on the first surface I found to fuck you, but it is all too dirty."

I snorted, looking at his disappointed frown. Before I could suggest cleaning something quickly, he turned me around in his arms. My legs surrounded his hips as his hands supported my bottom. My hands went up to his shoulders as a laugh bubbled up from his eagerness.

"This will work," Grant said as he unbuttoned his pants and pulled my skirts up.

"Oh, Grant," I moaned as his cock pushed at my entrance.

"It is custom for newlyweds to fuck when they enter their home for the first time," he said.

I had never heard of this custom before, but I did not care as long as I felt his cock inside of me again. He let gravity do most of the work as he let me sink down on his length. I moaned as he filled me, my legs spread wide to encompass his hips.

I could not do much more than let him take the lead as his massive cock filled me. My legs hung in the air as my hands gripped his shoulders tight. Grant pulled me up again, letting me fall down on his cock until my pleasure bud touched his groin. I moaned as pleasure sparked deep inside of me, his cock touching a spot deeper than he ever touched before.

As he pulled me up, almost sliding entirely out of me, my pussy squeezed around him as if trying to keep him inside. Grant groaned as he dropped me down again, filling me with all of him. He increased his pace, bouncing me on his cock, his powerful arms lifting me up again and again as if I weighed nothing.

"You feel so good around me," Grant groaned.

Pleasure rose as I helplessly moaned in his arms. He was using my body for his own pleasure, and I loved every second of it. He pulled my body closer to his, my pleasure bud trapped between us as his lips came to my neck. His tusks grazed my throat as he kissed and licked my delicate skin.

His movements rubbed my pleasure bud as his cock pleasured my pussy. I could feel my climax rise steadily with each thrust of his hips and lift of his arms. His groans became louder as his cock throbbed inside of me, signaling his impending release.

"My amazing wife," Grant groaned as he fucked me harder until pleasure overwhelmed me.

My pussy clenched around his cock as he came with a loud cry of pleasure. He filled me with his hot cum as pleasure washed over me. My own orgasm felt powerful and all-consuming as pleasure took over my senses. While his throbbing cock pulsed inside me, my legs spasmed. My body trembled as he held me close to him, his heart beating a thousand miles a minute as his cock throbbed deep inside of me.

"My wonderful husband," I murmured with my head on his shoulder.

"I love you so much, my little flower," Grant said.

I pulled my head back to look into his eyes and saw his love shine brightly.

"I love you too."

The End

Epilogue

A *few years later*

I was mending clothes when Grant entered our house holding a letter with my family's emblem on it.

"A letter from your sister," he said as he handed it to me and went to check on our baby.

"Oh, look Grant. She is to marry an Earl," I said while reading the letter from Lilly.

"I hope she finds happiness with him," Grant said, sitting next to me.

"How is Dahlia?" I asked.

"Fast asleep," Grant said as he pulled me onto his lap. "Are you still happy you married a lowly stable hand instead of someone with a grand title?"

"Very," I said with a smile. "I could not have wished for a better husband and father. Maybe I should show you how happy I am with our marriage?"

I slid off his lap, kneeling in between his legs. Grant groaned low as I opened his pants, his cock already hardening for me.

"Every day with you is a gift that I cherish with all my heart," he said.

His cock was too big to fit in my mouth, but I knew of other ways to pleasure him. I grabbed him with a firm grip as I licked at his tip. Grant bit back his groans of pleasure, trying not to wake our daughter as I caressed his cock. I let my lips drag down the side of his cock, licking every vein I encounter as I let one of my hands slip lower until I encompassed his heavy balls.

Grant panted as his hips thrust upwards, sliding his cock in my hand. I loved watching his face contort in pleasure, to see him biting his lip and his tusks pushing outward. Massaging his balls, I licked his cock head, earning me another strangled groan of pleasure.

We needed to be quiet, but I loved teasing him, trying to coax as many sounds out of him as possible. He was absolutely magnificent, towering high above me, his hands clenching into fists as groans tumbled from his throat. Arousal coursed through me as I looked at the Orc that was completely mine.

I gripped his cock tight, caressing him with firm strokes as I gently sucked on the tip. I could feel his cock throb underneath my hand, so close to bursting already. After a few more caresses, his whole body trembled as he came with a quiet groan. His seed spurted out, filling my mouth with his rich flavor. I eagerly swallowed down his release, but like always, it was too much for me to drink up. Some of it leaked out from my mouth as he came wave after wave.

"Delicious," I moaned as I licked the remains of his release from his cock.

"Gods, I love you," Grant groaned as he pulled me up in his lap and kissed me.

I moaned into the kiss, loving the way his tongue played with mine as if trying to memorize my taste. He pushed up my skirts, feeling between my legs and groaning when he found me wet and aching for him. Giving him pleasure gave me pleasure as well, and my pussy was ready for him. He let one meaty finger slip inside, testing the waters. I moved my hips to encourage him to give me more, and with a low rumble, he pulled his finger back and put his cock in its place.

"Ride me, my wife," Grant murmured as he helped me sink down on his cock.

I bit my lip to keep my moans inside as his cock filled my pussy like it belonged there. It was easier since giving birth, yet still so pleasurable to have his massive cock inside of me. His hands were around my hips, helping me bounce on his cock, sparking pleasure with each thrust. I touched him everywhere I could. His face, shoulders, and broad chest were all mine to touch and do with as I please. Some days, it was hard to believe he was truly mine forever. I could not imagine a better husband or father to our half-Orc daughter.

"I love you, Grant," I moaned as pleasure rose inside of me. "So, so much."

"I love you too, my wonderful wife," Grant groaned, increasing the pace of his thrusts, pushing me towards that high only he could give me.

I leaned forward, my lips on his neck as his hands and hips did all the work. His earthy, salty taste filled my mouth as I licked his neck on the spot which made him go crazy. We knew each other's body so well after our years of marriage, always searching for new ways to increase the other's pleasure. He growled low as he slid one hand in between us, locating my pleasure bud.

Grant circled it slowly with one finger as he kept the even thrusts of his cock. He was a master at playing with my body to wring as much pleasure out of me as possible.

"You feel so good around my cock," Grant growled, knowing that his words only spurred me on. "I love your pussy squeezing me as you take your pleasure from me."

My pussy clenched around his cock as if in response to his words, earning me a strangled groan from him. His hips moved faster than his finger, making smaller circles around my pleasure bud. I could feel my pleasure rise inside of me, so close to my climax already.

"I love your pussy, I love your heart, I love your mind," Grant growled, increasing his pace.

I could feel his cock throb inside of me, so close to his own climax, but he was determined to get me there first.

"Come for me, my little flower," Grant said as his finger flicked over my pleasure bud.

"Oh Grant," I moaned as he ignited my climax.

Pleasure washed over me as my pussy squeezed around his cock. He growled low as his hips stuttered and I could feel his cock throb deep inside of me, releasing his seed. Waves of pleasure flowed through me as he filled me with his release. Our climaxes mingled and the hushed sounds of our pleasure filled our small cabin.

My body trembled as my mouth closed around the skin of his neck, muffling my cries of pleasure. Grant's arms came around me, holding me close to his shivering body as he emptied his cock inside of me.

We both came down from our high slowly until our daughter started to cry. With a laugh and a kiss, I entangled myself from my husband to check on Dahlia, the little treasure we had created together. I was hoping for another treasure to come soon to join our growing family, but I needed to be sure before I could tell Grant.

The End

Marrying the Minotaur
The Proposal

I was looking for a husband. My criteria were simple. He needed a good title and have the ability to fill me with a child quickly, preferably a boy that could carry on my family's name.

My situation would have been different if my older sister hadn't run off to marry for love with our stable hand, but I knew she was happier. I wished I could marry for love, but I needed to marry in a way that would bring our family out of the ruins she had brought us in. Our name was scarcely worth anything, and my introduction into society was met with many raised eyebrows. But none of that mattered when I could arrange for a good husband myself.

My father was no use. After the failure he dealt with for trying to marry Violet off to an old Lord, he had withdrawn himself completely. I scarcely saw him anymore as he was always somewhere doing Gods knows what.

I scanned the ballroom, aware of the limited time I had. The season was almost over, and so far no man had approached me. I knew I had to make my move tonight and pick out a husband before it was too late.

My eye fell on a handsome Minotaur that stood to the side, observing people. I heard many tales about the virility of Minotaurs so that was already one thing on my list. I nudged my chaperone for the evening and subtly pointed to the Minotaur.

"Who is that?" I asked, sure I hadn't seen him at any of these balls before.

As a matter of fact, most of the balls were strictly human, with perhaps a Gargoyle or Satyr mixed in. Society liked to claim inclusiveness but was appalled when species crossed, which made it even more interesting for me. What better way for people to forget the scandal my sister had created than creating one myself?

"Oh, that is the Earl of Essington. He is new to society. He received his title and lands from the King after saving his life during a hunt last month."

My eyebrows raised as I took in the information. So he was honorable, had a good title, and great standing with our King. Seemed like he checked off all the boxes on my list. I thanked my chaperone and made my way around the ballroom. I chatted with everyone I passed as I kept my eyes on him. He seemed oblivious as to who was approaching him. His eyes focused on the dancing people, holding a long-forgotten glass in his hand.

When I reached him, I gently touched his shoulder, his eyes immediately fixing its gaze on me. I made a curtsy and offered my hand, but he didn't take it. I ignored my wounded pride and smiled up at him.

"Enchantée, my Lord. I do not think I have had the pleasure of making your acquaintance."

"I don't think we have," he said as he eyed me in a manner that was wholly improper and made heat rise to my cheeks.

"I am Lady Bennet," I said with a curtsy.

"I'm Ian," he said, not even mentioning his title.

It was obvious he was new to all this and didn't know or care about proper etiquette. In a way, it was refreshing to have someone who hadn't thought about his words five times before continuing the conversation.

"Well, then you can call me Lilly. I have but one question for you and I will no longer disturb you."

Ian angled his whole body towards me, his massive frame towering high above me and his impressive horns casting a shadow across the floor.

"I'm listening."

"Are you in need of a wife, my Lord?" I asked, just as he raised his glass for a sip.

He choked on the drink, and a mischievous smile played on my lips. After a loud cough and a sound that was every bit the animal he was part of, he looked at me.

"Excuse me?" he asked.

"Oh, you are certainly excused, my Lord. I was merely asking if you were in need of a wife. If not, I will be on my way again."

Before I could walk away, his hand grabbed my arm, and he pulled me back.

"I did not say I am not," he said. "You merely surprised me with your boldness."

"I need to be bold if I am to get what I want."

"And that is a husband?"

"Indeed," I said with a nod, as I looked at the ungloved hand that was still holding my naked arm.

It was entirely improper for him to continue touching me like that, but I could not find it in myself to tell him to let go. His hand felt warm and rough against my chilled, soft skin.

"I feel like this conversation should be held in private, do you not, lady Bennet?" Ian asked as he finally released my arm and offered me his in return. "Would you like to take a walk in the garden? It is a lovely evening."

I accepted it without question. I knew I should probably ask my chaperone to accompany us, but I could not find it in myself to care for it at that moment. If I were to speak freely and ask him to become my husband, I would rather not have anyone listening in on the conversation.

He escorted me to the garden, my hand on his arm and his hand on mine. The evening wind was chilly, but with his warm presence beside me, I did not feel cold.

"Now tell me, Lilly. Why should I marry you?" Ian asked.

His boldness surprised me less this time, but it was still hard to answer such a straightforward question without blushing. I took a deep breath, looking at the garden before me. I knew that if I looked into his gorgeous eyes, I would stumble over my words or my own feet, and that would not help my cause.

"I am from a good name. I can help you manage social gatherings. You have a title but no social standing as of yet. I know you can manage your lands, but I could help you manage your social calendar and your household."

"And what do you get out of it?" Ian asked as he stopped behind a bush where no one could see us, but I could still hear the party.

"A husband, and a title."

"Why me?" Ian asked. "I am sure you have many suitors."

I looked up at him and contemplated being honest with him.

"I do not have any worthwhile suitors since my sister married below our standing two years ago. I believe you have kind eyes, and I heard Minotaurs breed easily."

His eyes burned bright with passion as he made a wholly sensual sound, a low rumble of desire. The raw noise made a shiver wash over me and my insides clenched.

"So children would be part of the deal?" he asked.

"Yes. We would need a male heir sooner rather than later."

My Father was old and without a male heir. I was afraid my family's lands would fall into the wrong hands. I had to safeguard my legacy and my younger sister, who was set to be introduced to society next year.

Ian nodded, his giant horns swaying in the dark night, the candlelight reflecting off them. "I accept on one condition."

"Of course. What is your condition?" I asked, not surprised that he would have something to add to the arrangement.

"I get to have you in my bed every night and we will be husband and wife in every sense of the word. We will live together, eat together, and sleep together," Ian said, his voice low and husky.

My heart fluttered as I realized what his words meant. It would not be as simple as getting pregnant as quickly as possible. He wanted all of me for as long as I lived. Looking into his eyes again, I realized I wanted that as well.

"I accept."

The Wedding

It was a matter of days for everything to be arranged and before I knew it, I stood before the altar next to my soon-to-be husband in a gorgeous white dress. A mix of people, monsters, low and high born filled the church. A huge part of society came to witness our wedding as if it was some spectacle to watch.

The only comforting presence was my youngest sister behind me. Daisy had expressed her disdain for my decision but had supported me every step of the way. She had been with me during dress fittings, flower arrangements, and even when I contemplated running away.

All of my worries disappeared as I looked into the gorgeous blue eyes of the Minotaur that I would call my husband soon. The black fabric did not hide his bulging muscles. He towered high above me as if he could crush me with little effort, but in his eyes, I could see the same nerves reflected in them. We were practical strangers, but in moments marriage would unite us and our lives together would begin.

As he took my hands in his, I felt a calmness fill me. This might be a match made out of necessity, but I felt like our marriage could grow into something more. I had always been the romantic one of my sisters, dreaming of the day a man would sweep me off my feet, and I truly believed Ian could be that monster for me.

With two words, I sealed my fate, and suddenly his face descended on mine. I squeaked when his lips touched mine, earning a low rumbled laugh from him. And so we were husband and wife.

The Wedding Night

It felt like the wedding party flew by and we were suddenly alone in his bedroom. It was a grand room with a massive bed, fit for a Minotaur. I knew what was expected of me, and with a trembling hand, I undid my garment.

"Let me help," Ian rumbled low as he stepped behind me, his hooves thudding heavily on the wooden floor.

I let my hands drop, forcing myself to breathe steadily. With gentle movements he undid button after button, revealing my naked back in the warm air of the room. I was happy for the fire blazing in the fireplace or I would surely be shivering.

Ian caressed my naked back with the knuckles of his hand and a shiver washed over me, but it wasn't from the cold.

"So soft, pure, and perfect and all mine," Ian murmured.

"Yes, my husband," I whispered.

The word foreign in my mouth, but right for this moment. Ian was now my husband, and I was his wife and I had my marital duties to perform. But there was still one question stuck in my head that I had to ask before I could continue with our wedding night. When he unbuttoned the last in the row, I turned around, holding up the dress, before the fabric could drop away.

"I have a question for you, my Lord."

"Ian," he rumbled. "Don't call me by my title. Call me by my name."

I bowed my head. "Apologies my l- Ian," I said. "I merely wished to know why you accepted so quickly."

"Your proposal?" Ian asked.

I nodded. It had needed almost no convincing on my part. At the time I had felt relief at finally having a solution for my problem, but now I wondered how it came to be so easy for him.

"Because you made a fair point," Ian said as he took a step back and unbuttoned his dress shirt. "I have no interest in the social part of having a title, but I knew I had to partake or the King might take it away. But the real reason I said yes was because it meant having a beautiful, willing woman in my bed every night. And the truth is that I am bored with all the things I need to do and I cannot wait to have you underneath me every chance I get."

Another shiver washed over me with his honest, husky words. He pulled off the shirt, letting it fall on the floor. A shiny dark brown fur covered his entire torso, and my hands were itching to touch him.

"I see," I said, my voice breathless.

His hands went to his trousers, unbuttoning them with quick and efficient movements. In moments, he would be naked in front of me. My breathing sped up, and I could feel my insides clench. I've never seen a man or monster naked before and I couldn't seem to tear my eyes away from the bulge in his pants.

It was as if he knew the anticipation was building inside of me as he dragged down the fabric to reveal his cock. I gasped as I saw it for the first time. It was magnificent, covered in the same fur as his body, except for the tip that was round and pink, leaking a clear fluid. I licked my lips on instinct, wondering how he would taste.

"Do you wish to touch me, my wife?" Ian asked, and I nodded, unable to tear my gaze away from his massive member.

He walked towards me, his cock swaying with each step, mesmerizing me. I got down on my knees so it was eye level with me. I stretched out my hands, touching his bulging legs and stomach before I even dared to get closer to his cock. He felt so hot and firm underneath me. All muscles and strength, trembling to control himself.

"Have you ever touched a male before?" Ian asked.

I shook my head, still not ready to touch his cock. It looked frighteningly big, and I had no idea how it would ever fit inside of me.

"You need not worry, my wife. We will go slow. We have all of our lives ahead of us to discover each other," Ian said in a surprisingly gentle tone.

I looked up and remembered how kind his eyes had been when we first met, making me confident about this union. His eyes were blazing with lust, but also a kindness I hadn't expected on our wedding night. He wouldn't just take me like a ravenous beast, he gave me room to explore.

"How do I make you feel good?" I asked as I touched his cock for the first time.

It jumped under my touch, startled I pulled my hand back.

"Whatever you do will feel good," Ian groaned. "I have imagined your soft hands on me so many times already."

"You did?" I asked as I grasped his cock with a trembling hand.

It throbbed hot underneath my fingers, as if ready to burst at any moment.

Ian nodded. "I never imagined wedding and bedding someone as beautiful and soft as you. But after your proposal, I could not get you out of my head. The days it took for this wedding to be arranged were the longest of my life."

"Truly?" I asked, unable to imagine him as such.

"Is it so hard to believe that I lusted after you?"

"I do not-"

Ian grasped my hand on his cock, moving it with strong and sure caresses. "Is my hard cock not a testament to my words? I assure you, it will not grow this hard for just anyone."

A shiver washed over me as I could feel his hot, unyielding meat underneath my hands. It was too big for my fingers to wrap around, but his massive hand encompassed it with ease. Every part of him was so much larger than me.

"How... How will it fit?" I asked, breathless.

"We will need to make sure you are wet and ready to receive it. Have you ever touched yourself and made your pussy slick with need?"

I gasped at his crude words, shaking my head in denial. It wasn't proper for a lady to touch herself, but curiosity had gotten the better of me on rare occasions. Feeling his hard cock underneath my hand and seeing how much pleasure he gained from our joined stroking was making me feel aroused in a way I had never experienced before.

"Then I will need to show you how much pleasure there is to gain from it, my wife. I want your pleasure as much as I want mine," Ian said as he released his cock.

He took a step back, so I had to let go of him as well, both of us breathing heavily.

"Should we not... finish you?" I asked.

Ian shook his head as his breathing slowed down. "I want the first time I spend to be inside of you, my wife."

My core clenched at his words, already imagining how it would feel. We may not need to do much more to get me slick with need, as I could already feel wetness gather between my legs. Seeing my husband naked and aroused was doing things to my body I never thought possible.

"Get naked and on the bed," Ian said, his voice hoarse with need.

I obeyed immediately. Standing up, I let the beautiful white dress pool at my feet. His eyes devoured me and I could feel arousal course through me. Never taking my eyes off him, I took a step back. And another, and another until I could feel the bed hit the back of my knees. I sat down on the massive bed, crawling until I lay in the middle of it, naked and ready for my husband.

"Beautiful," Ian murmured as he crawled on the bed behind me.

His massive frame crowded me, blocking out the light of the fireplace. His horns loomed over me, dangerously sharp and monstrous, but my fingers were itching to touch them.

As if he could read my mind, he dipped his head lower until our mouths were only a hair's breadth away.

"Grab my horns," Ian growled.

My hands went upwards, closing around his light brown horns. They were big, hard, and textured underneath my fingers.

"Guide me to where you want me," Ian said.

"They are so big," I said as I let my hands travel all the way upwards to the tip.

"You flatter me, my wife. A Minotaur's horns are his greatest pride and joy and for you to compliment them, means the world to me. Now use them to guide me over your body."

I admired how he gave me control over him as if it was the most natural thing in the world. I couldn't put into words how I felt or what I wanted, but guiding his head to where I needed him with his horns seemed easy to me.

I pulled his head down until our mouths touched, our first kiss since the wedding. Our mouths were different, his much wider than mine, but somehow we fit together. His lips were warm and soft against mine. He held still, giving me time to explore until I let my tongue slip out to lick his lips. Ian groaned into the kiss, opening his mouth and letting his tongue come out to play as well.

This was how a kiss should be between husband and wife behind closed doors. The way his tongue plundered my mouth was not fit for the public, but perfect for the privacy of our bedroom. His tongue felt so big and delicious in my mouth. He tasted like brandy and the woods combined in one delicious cocktail.

When I felt like I couldn't take another breath, I pulled back. We were both breathing heavily, our eyes focused on each other, and the lust I could see in his made me gasp. This was just the beginning of our wedding night and I knew that there was still so much more to discover.

I guided his head lower until his hot breath fanned over my naked breasts. My nipples were hard and aching, begging for his mouth. His lips grazed my breast, and I gasped, tightening my grip on his horns. He didn't need any further encouragement, kissing my breasts. I moaned when his hot lips made contact with my overheated skin. My eyes closed without me realizing it, but Ian growled.

"Eyes open and on me, my wife."

I immediately opened them again, looking at my Minotaur husband, kissing my breasts. It felt so good I might burst, but he eased me into it. He placed slow and gentle kisses over my skin, ignoring my aching nipples. I never imagined it could feel this good, but I wanted him where I ached. I moaned, directing his head with his horns to my nipple.

He chuckled lightly, his hot breath fanning my nipple, making it pucker even more.

"Do you want me here, my wife?" Ian asked as he dropped a feather-light kiss on one of my nipples.

"Yes, please," I moaned as I nodded.

"As you wish," Ian said and flicked his tongue over my nipple.

My back arched as pleasure throbbed from that spot. His hot tongue didn't stop licking my hard nipple until I was panting and almost ready to beg him. I wasn't sure if I would beg him to stop or never stop, but he seemed to know my limits better than I did. He switched breasts and gave the exact same treatment to my other nipple.

"So good," I moaned as he switched again and again until I was a sweaty, panting mess of desire.

"But not good enough to make you come?" Ian asked as he slowly kissed down over my belly to where I was aching the most.

I didn't know what to answer, because I didn't know what this feeling was. Luckily, he seemed to know what I needed without me having to say it. My grip on his horns relaxed as his head went down over my body, kissing every piece of skin that he encountered.

I opened my legs so he could get in between them, averting my gaze as I saw how he looked at my pussy. It was as if I was a water well at the end of a long road and he was parched beyond saving.

"Look at me, my wife, and hold my horns steady. If I do something you do not find pleasing, just pull at them and I will stop."

I nodded, unable to imagine him doing something unpleasing after he had already shown me so much pleasure. As I looked at him again, I could not stop the moan that came from me. Ian looked as if he was going to devour me alive, and I was all too happy to let him.

He opened his mouth and I could see his big, meaty tongue come from his mouth. It was wider than my hand and the most delectable shade of pink that was in such a stark contrast with the rest of him. He licked me, and pleasure sparked like never before. It almost felt like he had touched all my pleasure points in one lick with his massive tongue.

Ian rumbled something against my pussy and started to devour me in all earnest. My hands tightened around his horns, needing something to hold on to as he rocked my world. His hands grabbed my legs when I threatened to close them around his head. My husband held me steady as his tongue did things to me I could have never imagined. Pleasure built up inside of me until I felt like I would burst and I begged him to stop.

"Push me away if you must, but I know you are almost there, Lilly. Let go and feel the pleasure," Ian rumbled before his head dove in between my legs again.

I wanted to push him away, but my body didn't seem to listen. The buildup became bigger and bigger and his tongue never left me until it became too much, and I came with a pleasured cry. Wave after wave of pleasure washed over me as my body trembled and my pussy clenched around nothing. It was the most wonderful feeling in the world and I could not believe he shared this with me. It felt like a gift between us, and I couldn't wait to share this pleasure with him.

Somewhere in my bliss, I had released his horns, my hands clenching the sheets instead. My back arched off the bed as pleasure consumed my senses. My husband made an unholy sound as he lapped up my release and caressed my trembling legs.

"You did well, my wife. How do you feel?" Ian asked as he pulled away from my achingly empty, but satisfied pussy.

"Boneless," I sighed.

Ian chuckled low as he crawled on top of me. "Not too tired for the act of matrimony, I hope?"

"There is more?" I asked.

"So much more. There is a world of pleasure I wish to show you."

"Then I am not too tired, my husband. Show me this world of pleasure," I said as I threw my arms around his wide neck.

"With pleasure," Ian rumbled as he kissed me.

He tasted different from before. His earthy flavor had a hint of tanginess, giving him an enjoyable taste. He pulled one of my legs over his hip, opening me wide for him. He presented his massive cock at my entrance and looked at me.

"This will only hurt for a moment. Please trust me," Ian said just before he pushed inside.

He was too big, too much, too wide for me. A sob escaped me as a slash of pain burst through my pleasure bubble. Ian murmured sweet words of encouragement as he pulled back and thrust back inside, trying to fit more of him in my pussy. I should have told him to stop, but I trusted his promise of pleasure.

After a few more thrusts, he completely penetrated me, filling me like I've never been filled before. He held still, letting me get accustomed to his invasion of my body. I tried to focus on everything else but the pain. I noticed how his chest was close to my nose and I could smell his raw, natural scent. I could feel and hear him take deep breaths as if trying to maintain control. Stretching out my hands to caress his fur, calmed me, and slowly my body relaxed as well.

"How do you feel?" Ian asked in a strained voice.

I looked up and saw how his face contorted with pleasure. He was holding himself still for me. Giving me time to adjust before he would ravish me like a beast and that realization made me warm inside.

"Good, please move," I said in earnest.

The height of the pain subsided and when he pulled out and thrust back inside again, pleasure took its place. I moaned when I could feel his cock touch every pleasure point inside of my pussy, sparking pleasure with each outward and inward motion.

"Fuck, so tight, so good. Best pussy in the fucking world," Ian grunted as he fucked me.

His crude words made heat rise in my cheeks but also in the rest of my body. He may be an Earl in name, but he was still just a monster at heart.

"Yes," I moaned. "So good."

"All mine. Mine to fuck as I please. I want to eat this pussy every day and fuck it every chance I get," Ian grunted.

"Yes, all yours, Ian."

"Lilly," he groaned. "Say my name again. Scream it when you come."

"Ian, Ian, Ian," I repeated his name like a prayer as he fucked me within an inch of my life.

"My beautiful, gorgeous wife," Ian groaned.

I could feel the pleasure rise inside of me, and recognized the feeling from before. It wouldn't be long before I came. It felt too good to have his cock inside of me and his massive body on top. I wanted to say something, warn him, but it was too late. I screamed his name in pleasure as my climax washed over me.

My pussy squeezed around his massive cock, igniting his orgasm as well, and he came with a heavy bellow. His cock throbbed, and he spurted his seed inside of me. My body trembled, but his massive body held it steady. The sounds of pleasure he made vibrated through the room and imprinted in my mind forever. My pussy milked his cock from its release as he gave me a last thrust, his body trembling to keep him upright.

When he finished the last of his release, he pulled out and rolled next to me. An obscene amount of his cum gushed out of me, ruining the sheets, but I could not make myself care about that when my whole body was limp with pleasure. He pulled me into his embrace, his soft fur shiny with sweat.

"That was marvelous," Ian rumbled.

I mumbled in agreement, feeling my eyes close in exhaustion. I could not have asked for a better, more caring husband than Ian.

The Honeymoon

I woke up to my husband in between my legs, lapping at my pussy as if it was his breakfast. I moaned and my hands went to his horns on instinct. He rumbled in reply, pushing his tongue inside of me, igniting my orgasm. My pussy clenched around his massive tongue as waves of pleasure washed over me.

I screamed his name as my climax ripped through me, my hands holding onto his horns. He pulled out his tongue, lapping up my juices as I came down from my unexpected morning treat.

"That was…"

"My breakfast," Ian said with a massive grin on his face.

I made a very unladylike sound in response, which made him laugh.

"What about my breakfast?" I asked, making his laughter stop in seconds.

"Hmm, what do you wish for breakfast?" Ian asked, looming over me.

My nerves got the better of me and instead of asking for his cock as I had intended, I asked for something easier. "A kiss."

"As you wish," Ian said, kissing me.

I moaned against his mouth, his taste mingled with mine in a delicious cocktail. His tongue touched mine, fucking my mouth much as he had done to my pussy only moments ago. As he pulled back, I could feel his cock rest heavily on my thigh, hard and throbbing.

"Is that all you wish for breakfast, my wife?" Ian asked, his eyes shining bright with lust.

I shook my head, unable to put into words what I wanted, but he seemed to know what I needed.

"Turn around," Ian said as he grabbed a pillow.

I got on my knees, and he pushed the pillow underneath my hips, elevating them higher. I could hear and feel him come up behind me, his immense body covering my back. One hand was on my hip and he used the other to position his cock at my entrance. I was wet and ready from my orgasm, but I could still feel it burn as he pushed inside of me.

I moaned as he slowly gave me inch after inch of his amazing cock. He felt even bigger in this position, filling me to the brink. His heavy breaths ruffled my hair as his fur tickled my back.

"Such a sweet pussy," Ian groaned. "So tight, and wet, and all mine."

"Yes, please, fuck me," I moaned, braver now that I couldn't see his face.

"Fuck yes, Lilly. I will fuck you every time you ask, my sweet wife," Ian said as he pulled back and thrust inside of me again, sparking pleasure deep inside.

My pussy was already clenching around his cock, still sensitive from my first orgasm of the day. His hips moved faster, pounding his cock in my pussy, touching something deep inside of me I'd never felt before. Before I could even know what happened, my climax ripped through me. A scream of pleasure tore from my throat as my pussy clenched around his cock.

"Milk my cock, Lilly. Yes, so good," Ian groaned as I could feel his cock throb inside of me.

My pussy milked his cock as pleasure washed over me. After a few more thrusts, he came with a strangled roar, filling my pussy with his seed. Pump after pump, he filled me with his seed. So much more than my pussy could take. I could already feel it leaking out before he was even finished coming. With a shivering cry, he gave me the last of his release. His massive body slumped over me, held upright by his muscular arms to not crush me with his weight.

With a groan, he pulled out and fell next to me. The sheets were definitely ruined, but all I cared about were his warm arms surrounding me, pulling me against his chest. We both smelled like sweat and sex, but with my body still humming with pleasure, it did not matter.

"My amazing, wonderful wife," Ian murmured against my hair.

I hid my smile against his chest, not sure how to respond to his praise. We both found pleasure in the act, so I was not opposed to doing this every day for the rest of my life.

When I had caught my breath and felt like I could move my body again, I lifted my head.

"Let us clean ourselves and start on our day," I said.

"Do we have to?" Ian asked. "Can we not just stay in bed all day and have sex until the night falls?"

I laughed as he pouted at me like a child begging for a sweet.

"I would like to have a look at the property and see what needs to be done."

"We can do that tomorrow as well. We are newlyweds, Lilly. Everyone expects us to fuck like animals."

I could feel my cheeks heat up, realizing everyone expected us to fornicate. "We should at least eat."

"That is something I can get behind. Fuel for our activities," Ian said as he kissed me. "Stay and do not get dressed. I will return with food."

Ian got out of bed and I got a first look at the naked behind of my husband. His ass was absolutely delicious. It was firm, covered in the same short brown fur as the rest of him, with a cute tail tucked just above his ass cheeks.

He pulled on a pair of pants but dismissed a shirt. When he left the room, I fell on the sheets with a happy sigh. I could see this marriage working. We still needed to get to know one another, but I had a feeling our match was at least well-balanced in the bedroom.

Ian came back with some grapes and bread and we ate on the bed as if we were children having a sleepover. He was so relaxed and easygoing, easing my own nerves.

"I would really love to see your estate, my husband," I said when we finished our food.

Ian groaned. "Fine, but you cannot wear more than one item of clothing."

A blush caressed my cheeks, but I nodded. I got off the bed to put on the only thing I had in this room, but his hand stopped me. He presented me with his own shirt, which I happily accepted. It was far too big for me, hanging over my knees and even with the top button fastened, the swell of my breasts was still very much visible.

"I quite enjoy you in my clothes," Ian rumbled as his eyes roved over me.

"I quite like you without them," I said, averting my eyes.

A low laugh sounded from him, warming me from the inside out. "Let us go before I ravish you again, my wife."

I was not opposed to being ravished by him, but I truly wanted to see the estate that I had married into. As we walked around, he talked to me about the hunt where he had saved the life of the King. He attempted to make it sound like a menial thing, but as he described the wild beast he had to fight with his bare hands and showed the scar he got from it, I was impressed.

He had only used two rooms since moving in. All the other rooms still had protective sheets covering the furniture to keep the dust away. There were only two members of staff who had been with the house since the beginning.

"There is too much space. I would not even begin to know what to do with all of it. This manor has three dining rooms. Who in the world needs three dining rooms?"

"Well, you use the one corresponding with the stature of your guest," I said.

"Why not have them all in the same room?" Ian asked.

"That is not how it is done," I said.

"Maybe we should start doing things differently," Ian murmured. "For example. I would like my family to move into the East Wing."

I nodded. It was not unusual for the family of the Earl to live with him until they were married off. "How many rooms should we prepare?" I asked.

Ian shrugged. "I do not know. We used to live in a one-bedroom house."

"How many are there in your family?"

"My mother, my three sisters, and my two younger brothers. I am the oldest and, by gaining this title, I am able to give them a much better life than I had. "

"And you all lived in a one-bedroom home?" I asked.

"Yes. My father left us with debt and the only reason we could even afford that was because I worked for the King."

"I am certain we can all give them their own room in the East wing. This house is big enough."

"How does one even have a house this big? It is ludicrous," Ian said as we walked into yet another dining room.

I never saw it that way, but hearing how he lived in one small place with a family of seven, I could hardly imagine us living here alone.

"Property taxes," I said. "It has always been done this way, and it is how the King controls the lands."

"And now I have to," Ian said.

"With a title does come a certain level of responsibility, but I am sure you will be a fair landlord."

"I hope so. I am glad you will be able to assist me."

"Of course. I am your wife and I will be with you every step of the way."

"Do you want your family to move in too?" Ian asked.

"Oh, I would not imagine they will. My older sister married a stable hand and seems quite content with her life and growing family. My younger sister will be introduced to society next year. Thanks to our marriage, she will have many more prospects, and I am sure she will find a good husband."

He nodded as if lost in thoughts as we walked into a drawing room. The house seemed empty now, but I was certain with his family and hopefully, soon our own laughter would fill our house in no time.

"Do you know what having this many rooms means?" Ian asked with a smile.

We completed our tour, reaching the main dining room once more.

"I do not."

He turned around and picked me up, making me squeal with surprise.

"That we must make many babies to fill them with," Ian said. He put me down on the massive dining room table surrounded by tall windows overlooking the garden. "I think we should start here," he said as he pulled his shirt up, exposing my naked pussy to his gaze.

"Oh, yes, please, my husband," I moaned.

Arousal coursed through me and I could already feel wetness gather between my legs. It seemed that he needed to merely look at me with lust in his eyes to ignite my body for him.

"How do you want me?" Ian asked.

"What do you mean?" I asked, my pussy already gathering wetness and clenching in anticipation.

"Do you want my fingers, my tongue, or my cock?" Ian asked as his fingers traced my pussy.

"Would it be awfully improper to say I want all of you?" I asked.

"It is never improper to say that to your husband," Ian said with a grin as he got down on his knees in front of me. "And I am more than happy to oblige."

His massive tongue licked me, making my toes curl as one of his fingers entered. A moan tumbled from my lips as arousal and pleasure rose inside of me. The more I had of him, the more I seemed to crave him. He was an addiction I never even saw coming.

When I was sufficiently wet, he got up, pulled his pants down, and entered me in one thrust. His pleasured groan and my breathless moan filled the vast room as he pulled back and thrust inside of me again, and again. His cock sparked pleasure deep inside of me with each thrust.

"Grab my horns," Ian grunted.

My hands went up to grab his swaying horns as his hips moved quicker. I could already feel the pleasure rise inside of me and I knew it would not be long before I came. I wanted him to come with me and join me in my pleasure.

"You... you feel so good inside of me," I moaned.

"Fuck, Lilly, say that again," he groaned as his movement faltered.

"I... I love your big cock inside of me," I moaned, a blush creeping up my cheeks, but when I saw how wild his eyes became and how much faster his hips moved, I gained some confidence in my words. "I want you to fill me with your seed, and breed me."

That last part seemed to ignite something primal inside of him as he bellowed loud, his cock throbbing deep inside of me as he filled me with his seed. His massive body trembled on top of me as his release took over. I had not come yet, but I did not mind seeing my husband lost in his own pleasure, his face contorted with pleasure, biting his lip as his hips stuttered against mine.

Breathing heavily, he looked at me with desire burning in his eyes.

"That was the most arousing thing you could ever say," Ian said. "You made me lose control, coming before you."

Before I could answer, one of his hands was on my pussy, his meaty finger circling my pleasure bud. A moan tore from my throat as he teased it. His throbbing cock was still inside of me and I felt so full with his cum. It only took a few swipes before my pleasure washed over me and my pussy squeezed around his cock, earning a strangled groan from him.

He pulled out, stumbling on a chair, panting. He was truly a magnificent vision and all mine. I could not imagine my life without him, I suddenly realized.

"What is it, my dear wife?" Ian asked as he saw the look on my face.

I looked at him as a smile broke through. "I believe I am starting to fall in love with you."

He picked me up and twirled me around the room with a boisterous laugh. "That is the best thing I heard since the King granted me my title." He sat me down again, breathing hard. "I believe I am starting to fall in love with you too, my wife," Ian said and kissed me.

The End

Epilogue

A few years later

Children's laughter echoed throughout our house. Ian's family quickly became as close as my own and his mother helped me out during the pregnancy of our first child. I was feeding Rose when Ian entered with a formal-looking invitation.

"It seems that your sister is to marry a Duke," Ian said, handing me the invitation.

"Daisy?" I asked, dumbfounded.

I had worried for so many years about her marriage prospects, but she snagged herself a Duke. We had spoken only recently at our father's funeral and she had not even mentioned any courtship.

"Jealous that she managed to snag a Duke while you only married an Earl?" Ian asked with a wink.

I laughed, shaking my head. "No, merely surprised she never mentioned him before."

When our daughter had enough, I handed her to him, his eyes focused on my exposed breasts. "Do not cover those," he growled.

My husband lay Rose on her cot and she immediately went to sleep. Returning to me, he kneeled in front of me.

"My beautiful wife," Ian murmured, his eyes on my naked breasts. "How did I get so lucky?"

"By saving the King," I said.

"I am grateful for the beast we encountered that day."

"Me too," I said, caressing his cheek, letting my hands glide to his horns. "Because now I have a beast to call my own."

Ian bent over, kissing my breasts as I grabbed his horns to keep them from stabbing me. His lips and mouth did things to my breasts that made pleasure spark deep inside of me. I loved the feeling of his tongue on my naked skin and his warm breath leading the way.

Ian pulled the rest of my dress aside so he could go lower, over my belly, and in between my legs. He kissed every part of me he encountered, showing how much he loved my body even though it changed with my pregnancy.

"I love every inch of you," Ian growled as he opened my legs wide to lick my pussy. "So wet already."

His tongue licked my pussy with one firm stroke, moaning as my taste filled him. Pleasure sparked, but I felt achingly empty and I needed him to fill me.

"Yes, Ian, please," I moaned.

"I love seeing you swollen with my child. I need to fuck you, fill you with my seed, and breed you."

"Yes, my husband, breed me," I moaned as my hands tightened around his horns.

He picked me up as if I weighed nothing, and in two steps he was at our bed. He gently laid me down, caressing my face with such care that my heart felt full. This massive beast was all mine, and every day he showed me what love should feel like.

"Do you want my cock?" Ian growled as he pulled down his pants, freeing his magnificent cock.

"Yes, give it to me, now," I moaned.

"I love it when you demand my cock," Ian said as he positioned it at my entrance.

"I need your cock, I need my husband to breed me," I moaned.

He growled low, every bit the monster he was as he thrust inside of me with one push. A strangled sound left me as he filled my pussy with all of him. My hands went up to his horns again, grabbing the comforting hardness as his rock-hard cock fucked my pussy.

"Such a sweet pussy, and all mine," Ian growled.

"All yours, forever," I moaned.

His hips moved faster, fucking me with sure strokes, making pleasure rise inside of me. One hand slid in between us, circling my pleasure bud. He always wanted me to come first, and we made it into a little game to see who could make who lose control. I squeezed my pussy around his cock, feeling the pleasure spark inside of me and seeing it reflected on his face.

"Breed me, fill me with seed," I moaned while squeezing my pussy.

His eyes burned bright with desire, as he bit his lip and fucked me even harder, chasing my high together with his. His finger and his hips joined each other at a punishing pace, trying to make me come around his cock. We needed to be fast because our daughter tended to sleep in short intervals.

"Fuck Lilly, you feel too good," Ian groaned.

"Yes, so good, Ian," I moaned.

His hips stuttered and I could feel his cock throb inside of me, but I was close as well. A few more thrusts and I fell over the edge. He kissed me to swallow our moans as my pussy milked his cock of his release. His cock throbbed deep inside of me as he gave me spurt after spurt of his cum, filling my pussy. Pleasure filled me, making everything around me disappear.

Even though I married Ian for his title, I ended up loving every aspect of him, and I could have not asked for a better husband or father for our daughter.

The End

Marrying the Gargoyle
The Proposal

Men with ill intentions surrounded me. I didn't have any money or reputation to lose, so all I had to give was my life, which seemed less valuable with each passing day. It might not be worth much, but I would still fight with all I had to protect it.

The first man approached me, and I hit him square in the face with my balled-up fist. A sharp pang of pain shot through my hand and my arm, but I ignored it. That would only seem like a pinprick as opposed to what these men were planning to do with me.

Before the next man reached me, a dark shadow appeared above us. The air shifted as the flap of wings sounded through the small alley. With a whoosh, a gorgeous, purple Gargoyle landed before me. He took one look at the situation and made quick work of the men surrounding me. In moments, the men scattered, and I found myself alone with my Gargoyle savior.

"Thank you, my Lord," I said as I made a curtsy.

He grabbed my hand, careful not to nick me with his claws, and pulled me upright again. I got a good look at his face, and his beauty mesmerized me. His skin and the inside of his wings were the color of pale lavender and his horns and the hooks on his wings were a rich purple. His piercing green eyes seemed to look right into my heart as if he already knew me, but I would have remembered if we met before.

"No need to bow for me," he rumbled in a delicious voice that did things to my body I had never experienced before.

"I was not bowing. I was curtsying," I said, not able to withstand the need to correct him.

"What is the difference?" he asked.

"Men bow, woman curtsy," I said.

"I see," he said with a faint smile grazing his purple lips.

His stone-cold hand was still in mine and the differences between us fascinated me. I had heard tales about Gargoyles and how they came into existence, but I've never had the pleasure of meeting one.

"What-"

"How-"

We both started asking our questions at the same time and broke off with a laugh. He bowed his head to me and raised my hand slightly.

"Ladies first," he said.

"Oh, no. I do not think my question is appropriate for this time of night," I said.

I usually spoke before thinking, and now that I had the time to evaluate my question, I realized how improper it was.

"Now you have only fueled my interest," he said.

"Please, do go first. I promise I will ask my question after answering yours."

"If you so please," he said with a nod. "I was going to ask, what a fine lady like you was doing here all alone at night."

"Oh, that is an easy question. My carriage broke down a few blocks back. Since my coachman lived close by where it happened, I told him to go home and that I was fine walking the last few blocks on my own."

I didn't tell him that our money was running out and I couldn't afford to get the carriage fixed or even pay the coachman his wage for next month.

"That does not seem safe," he said, his eyebrows raised. "A lady should always be escorted, especially in a neighborhood like this."

"Ah, but that would indicate I was a lady, and I am but an old spinster without any marriage prospects."

He shook his head as he still held my hand in his. "I would hardly think you were a spinster. What are you? Not even thirty?"

"You are too kind, dear sir," I said with a smile, although offended.

I was 27 but having been out in society for many seasons now and being the third daughter with two older sisters, both married to monsters, had made me anything but an ideal marriage candidate. That, paired with the fact I couldn't even afford new dresses for all the stupid balls where I might find a husband, made my situation rather fixed.

Considering my father died a few weeks ago, leaving me with nothing but debt and the next Lord of our estate overseas doing god knows what, I might as well be an old lady, resigning in my fate.

"There must be men lining up to ask for your hand," he said.

"I do not see any man around here except for you," I said and gently tried to pull my hand back, but his grip was like stone and I couldn't even budge him.

"You do not know me," he said.

"I do not," I said with a nod. "But you have just saved me from a group of men with ill intentions."

"What if I did that so I could have you all to myself?" he asked as his voice grew darker.

A shiver washed over my back, but it was not out of fear. "What would you do if you were to have me, my Lord?" I asked, raising an eyebrow.

He cleared his throat as if remembering what was proper. "Apologies, my lady. I do not believe I introduced myself."

He bowed, his wings stretching wide behind him, making him seem even larger than the street we were occupying. With gentle lips, he placed a soft kiss on the top of my hand. His lips were softer than I imagined, but as cold as his stony hand.

"I am the Duke of Everport."

I curtsied again, bowing my head lower as a sign of respect. I had not expected to encounter a Duke in this part of town, but I knew the proper way of addressing one.

"A pleasure, my Grace. I am Lady Bennet. The youngest of the Bennet sisters."

"Daisy Bennet," he said, and I angled my head up in surprise.

"Yes, how did you know?"

"I was flying towards your home when I saw the commotion."

"Why were you flying towards my home?" I asked.

I had no visitors since my father's passing a few weeks ago, and I should have known if he had been in business with the Duke of Everport.

"To propose marriage," he said.

For the first time in my life, I did not know what to say.

When I regained the ability to speak, all that came out of my mouth was the shrill sound of my voice. "Me?"

He nodded. "Your father had a great deal of debt in my account, and before he died, he offered me your hand in exchange."

I opened my mouth in outrage. I would not marry simply to settle a debt between men, but before I could speak, he continued.

"I refused at the time, giving him plenty of other possibilities of wiping away his debt, but he never did. I know how many debt collectors are coming to your door as soon as the mourning period is over, and I wanted to propose a deal. You become my wife and I settle every account still in your father's name."

"Why?" I asked, knowing a good deal when I heard one, but needing to know more before signing my life away.

"Because I am an old man with too much money and in desperate need of company. I promise our marriage will be in name only. I only require you to be on my arm for some social gatherings and your company during the weekly opera. Apart from that, you are free to go and do as you please."

I was the smartest of my three sisters, and I knew that an offer like this would come only once in a lifetime. It seemed that the house of Bennet would be filled with monsters after all. If my father knew, he would turn around in his grave, which only gave my decision a sweeter taste.

"I accept your proposal."

The Wedding

The arrangements took weeks. Apparently, the wedding of a Duke was the most talked about affair in the city and everyone wanted to be a part of it. I did not see my husband-to-be during this time, but I did feel his eyes on me when it was dark out and I was alone in my room. Every time I tried to find him, the feeling would disappear and I would be left feeling alone.

I hoped we would be able to get to know one another before marrying, but that hope seemed childish as the day of our wedding came closer. The only hope I clung to was that he would keep his promise of settling my father's debt, as I knew that our family's estate was in desperate need of repairs.

My sisters came over with their families to help me prepare for my wedding day in the cathedral. It felt like a lifetime ago that we saw each other, even though it was mere months since our father's passing.

"A Duke," Violet said with a laugh, caressing her growing belly. "However did you manage that, Daisy?"

"He saved my life," I said truthfully, not about to mention the debt our Father left me with.

Both my sisters were happily married and with children. There was no need to cause them any more stress to deal with by sharing a situation that would be rectified in a matter of weeks.

"I never thought I would see the day that our little sister marries," Lilly said with a smile as she helped me put a gorgeous tiara in my hair. It was a family heirloom from the Duke and the only sign of life he had given me in the past weeks. "I am so happy for you."

"Thank you," I said with a smile, even though I felt like I was suffocating.

I never wanted to be married, unlike my sisters, who had dreamed of it as a little girl. I just wanted to be free and study and consume knowledge, but suddenly I was in front of the cathedral surrounded by people, waiting for my soon-to-be husband to show up. As soon as dusk settled in, he flew inside with his magnificent wings spread wide.

Everyone gasped and pointed at him, but all I had eyes for was his face. He landed in front of me with a bow, taking my hands, and the ceremony started. The Bishop said his full name, and finally, I knew what to call my husband.

"Jacob," I whispered his name for the first time. "I do."

His eyes burned bright with lust, but he averted his gaze before I could truly see it. When the Bishop commanded us to kiss, he merely grazed my lips, pulling back before I could even have a taste of his mouth.

The cathedral exploded in applause as he presented us to society as husband and wife. People led me away to our wedding party, and I separated from my husband almost as quickly as he had entered. I was the wife of a Duke and a Duchess, but I've never felt so alone in my life.

The Wedding Night

The party had come to an end just before dawn. My husband escorted me upstairs, showing me to my room. As I turned around to thank him, he disappeared. With a sigh, I turned to the grand window and saw the first light appear. My wedding night was already over and the first day as a Duchess had begun.

I had no idea what my marriage would look like, but I had not expected my husband to avoid me. Days passed as I learned about his estate and met with all of his staff. Much was to be done as a Duchess, but it felt weird knowing we had not yet consummated our marriage.

As the sun set after a week of loneliness, I went on the mission of finding my husband. I searched every room in the house, at long last finding him in his study on the other side of the estate.

"Husband," I said and curtsied.

"Wife," Jacob said and acknowledged me with a nod. "I hope you have found your new home adequate."

"Yes, of course," I said as I stepped into the room, closing the door behind me. "Although it feels quite lonely without my husband by my side."

"I should have told you about my... lifestyle," Jacob said after a slight pause. "I am different in the way that I sleep like a stone during the day and work during the night. I have tried not to disturb you."

"You did not disturb me at all. It is just..."

I wasn't sure how to broach the subject without sounding wanton. So I opted for easier conversation. I looked around his magnificent study, admiring his grand collection.

"You have a fine collection of books, Your Grace. I was wondering if I could take my time studying them."

"Of course. Everything I own is yours as well."

Everything except his company, apparently. "Thank you."

I wandered around his study, looking at all the books lining his walls. There were more than I could ever read in a lifetime, but I was not afraid to try. I picked up a title I had been meaning to read for a while now and sat in the chaise closest to him.

"You will read here?" Jacob asked.

"If it is agreeable with you, Your Grace. You said everything you own is mine as well."

"Of course," Jacob said and focused his attention on the papers in front of him.

My curiosity and need for conversation got the best of me. "What are you doing?" I asked.

"Settling the last of your father's debt," Jacob said, not looking up from the papers.

"Oh, all of it?" I asked.

I knew how much my father had left me with, and I could not imagine him settling them so quickly.

"Yes, even the state of your sister's dowries."

"Their dowries?" I asked as I stood up from the chaise and approached his desk.

I had not gone that far back in my father's paper, imaging them paid or my sisters would have told me.

"He merely paid pennies when they are worth so much more."

"I must thank you, my Grace. I never imagined..."

"No need to thank me. I am merely righting the wrongs from the past."

"And what of the wrongs of the present?" I asked, unable to stop my lips from moving before I could think better of it.

"Which wrong do you speak of?" Jacob asked, his gaze lifting up to mine.

I stood as close to him now as I did at our wedding. "We have yet to consummate our marriage."

His eyes burned bright with passion before he averted his gaze. "I thought you understood the arrangement we had."

I took his hand and put it on my chest, his sharp claws pricking my skin. The cold and hard texture of his skin cooled my overheated skin.

"Arrangements can be altered," I whispered, suddenly feeling like my voice was too loud for the intimacy of our conversation.

"Only when both parties agree to it," Jacob said, avoiding my gaze.

"Do you not agree with me? Is it not the duty of a husband to see to his wife's needs?"

"I can arrange for..."

"I need you," I said, daring to step closer until my legs were against the desk and my body almost touched his. "I need my husband."

"Please, Daisy. Do not ask this of me."

It was the first time he said my name since our wedding and I couldn't wait to hear it again and again. "You married a woman of flesh and blood with needs."

Jacob pulled his hand back and stood up with such force his chair tumbled backward. His wings spread wide, causing the papers to fly off his desk.

"And you married a monster made of stone," Jacob hissed, extending his claws.

If he wanted, he could slice me in half with those, but I knew he wouldn't. He was more scared of hurting me than loving me.

"Please, your Grace, Jacob," I said, extending my hand out to him.

His wings shivered when I said his name.

"I could hurt you, scar you, break you," Jacob growled.

"I trust you," I said as I took a step forward, encouraged when he didn't back away.

"You are too soft and delicate," Jacob said as he touched a lock of my hair with his claw.

"I will not break. But my heart might if you keep avoiding me."

His eyes focused on mine, and the sorrow I saw in them almost broke my heart. He had been alone for so long, always afraid of hurting the people around him.

"I would never forgive myself if I harmed you."

"And I would never forgive myself if I did not do everything in my power to make this a successful marriage," I said, daring to take another step forward until I could touch his chest.

I could feel his heart beat strong inside of it. If he had a heart to give, I would gladly accept it, but I would start with gaining access to his body. He towered above me, such a grand creature, so scared of what he could do to me that he didn't even think of the possibilities of how good we could be together.

"Let me guide you."

Jacob let out a long, shuddering breath as his hand came over mine.

"How?"

"Sit back on the chair and let me touch you."

Jacob pulled the fallen chair back up and sat down on it with a heavy thunk. Nerves rattled through me, as I had no idea what I was doing. I had read many books and listened to the tales of maids, but I had never touched a man, let alone a monster, before.

I crawled on his lap, straddling his legs. He groaned when my fabric-covered pussy ground over his hardening erection. There were too many layers between us, but I needed to go slow. I touched his face, and he closed his eyes when my hands caressed his cheeks. I wanted to discover every inch of him and take my time touching him.

I moved higher to touch his horns, fascinated by the shape and feel of them. His hair was surprisingly soft for being made from stone, as I remembered his lips being. Slowly, I let my hand travel lower over his cheeks again, arriving at his beautiful mouth.

"Can I kiss you?" I asked as my thumb caressed his lower lip.

"Yes, please," Jacob groaned, eyes still closed.

I leaned closer, lightly touching my lips to his, and pulling back just as quickly. With a groan, he opened his eyes and licked his lips.

"Again."

Arousal coursed through me at his rough command. I was finally touching my husband, and he seemed to enjoy it. With a newfound confidence, I leaned in and kissed him again, more firmly this time. I had never kissed anyone before and in books, it always seemed like such a natural thing.

With a groan, he grabbed my head in his big hand and angled it so he could deepen the kiss. His tongue touched my lips, and I opened my mouth to let him inside. When his tongue touched mine, I moaned into the kiss. Jacob showed me how it was done, guiding me in the art of kissing as he took my breath away with his mouth.

My hands traveled lower over his chest as his mouth did things to me I had never even imagined. The kiss filled me with passion, longing and so much lust that I felt like I would explode if I didn't feel more of him. I could feel my pussy clench, achingly empty and ready to be filled by him.

With trembling fingers, I undid the buttons of his dress shirt, loving the way his marble chest felt underneath my hands. He seemed too engrossed in the kiss to notice my hand moving even lower. I needed to feel his cock and have it inside of me. We needed to consummate our marriage.

I pulled my skirts to the side as I opened his trousers. When my hand encompassed his cock, he broke the kiss to gasp and groan.

"Your hands," Jacob groaned as I gripped him tight.

Knowing he was made of stone, I confidently used a firm grip without the fear of hurting him. The tip was already leaking precum, and I knew I needed it to ease the way. I didn't dare look at it out of fear of losing my courage. It felt impossibly big in my hands, but I knew women were made to stretch.

Arousal coursed through me as I stroked his cock, using his precum to ease my movements. I pushed away my undergarments as I positioned myself on top of his cock.

"Daisy," Jacob moaned as the tip of his cock kissed my entrance.

I was wet with arousal, but I knew it would hurt. I preferred a quick pain over a lengthy one, so I let myself fall down on him, spearing me on his cock with one movement.

As pain shot through me, I couldn't help but gasp, but the way his eyes widened and the sound of pleasure he made added a thrilling intensity to the moment. His cock stretched me to my absolute limit, making it feel like he split me in half. I breathed through the pain, knowing, or rather hoping, pleasure would come soon after. Our temperature difference eased the pain slightly. My hot pussy clamped around his stone-cold cock as I grabbed his shoulders to keep me steady.

"My amazingly brave wife," Jacob murmured when I felt like I could breathe again.

"My husband," I said as I pulled up and let myself fall down again.

I could hear a scratching sound, and I saw that his claws were buried in the wooden armrests of his chair. The second downward thrust sent waves of pleasure coursing through me, intensifying the feeling. I gasped and repeated the movement over and over again until I was bouncing on his cock, pleasure growing inside of me.

The sounds I made didn't sound like my own as I rode my husband's cock. Everything around me ceased to exist as I found pleasure with my Gargoyle. My legs were burning with the exertion, but I knew he needed to be close by the sounds he made and how I could feel his cock throb deep inside of me.

"I will not last much longer," Jacob gritted out between his teeth. "Take your own pleasure first."

I had been so focused on his pleasure that I had scarcely thought of my own. Not many of the books I read had been focused on female pleasure. My movement faltered as I looked at my husband.

"Touch yourself between your legs. Find the pearl of pleasure and rub it," Jacob said, his hands still buried in the chair.

I pushed my hand underneath my skirt, trying to find something I had never heard of before. How would a pearl of pleasure feel? I felt his cock buried deep inside of me, twitching, while I searched for my pleasure point. As soon as my fingers touched the bud above my entrance, my pussy squeezed around him, earning me another guttural groan.

"That is it, my wife. Rub it until you feel like you will burst, and continue rubbing it until it happens."

I moaned as I rubbed the sensitive spot between my legs. How had I never known it was there? How had I lived so long without touching it? Now that I had found it, I didn't want to stop until I reached that climax so many books had described.

My pussy fluttered around his cock as I rubbed myself. The pleasure inside of me was building higher and higher, and it felt like it would become too much. Moans tumbled from my lips as my hips moved together with my fingers.

"Yes," Jacob groaned as his hips pushed up, deepening the thrusts. "Come for me, my beautiful, brave wife. Come around my cock."

His words unlocked something inside of me. As if my pleasure was something for me to claim and for him to enjoy as well. My movements sped up as the pleasure became even bigger. It was too much, too big, but I kept moving, chasing that high I had never experienced before with my husband's encouraging words leading me higher.

Just when I thought it couldn't possibly become bigger, it burst. With a pleasured cry, I could feel my orgasm wash over me. My pussy squeezed around him as my whole body trembled with my release. Jacob thrusts his hips up with abrupt movements, and suddenly I could feel his cock throb inside of me, spurting out his own release.

His wings shivered as his hips froze in an upward motion. Pleasure as I've never experienced before took over my body as my pussy milked his cock of his release. His gorgeous face contorted with pleasure, and it was the most beautiful thing I had ever witnessed.

"Daisy," he groaned as the last of the tremors left his body.

"Jacob," I said as I let myself fall down against his chest.

His purple wings surrounded us as he pulled his claws from the chair. "That was the most amazing experience ever."

"Hmm," I mumbled as I nestled closer to him. "Worth repeating, I hope?"

"I did not hurt you?" Jacob asked, fear lacing his voice now that pleasure wasn't addling his brain anymore.

I looked up and cupped his cheek. "Not even for a moment," I said.

"My courageous wife," Jacob said. "How did I get this lucky?"

"By betting with the wrong man, it seems."

A low chuckle made his cock move inside of me, and I moaned.

"Please let me take you to bed. You need your rest," Jacob said as he pulled me off his cock.

"What I need is a husband that will be by my side. I slept during the day so I could be with you during the night. But I would not be opposed to a bath."

"I will ring for a bath."

"Only if you will join me."

"I will."

I had already informed the maids we would need a bath when we emerged from his study, hoping my plan would have played out like this. By the time we reached the bathing room, there were already two hot and steaming tubs ready for us.

I could feel his seed trickling down my legs, and I knew it had ruined my undergarments, but I didn't care. I sent the maids away, needing to touch my husband more. Even his clothing fascinated me with an ingenious system of buttons around his wings for him to easily get freed. My hands lingered too long on his skin, but he didn't seem to oppose it.

After undressing, he turned around to me.

"Are you fond of that dress?" Jacob asked.

"Not particularly," I said, looking down at my simple blue dress.

"Good," Jacob growled and with one claw, he sliced it in two.

I gasped when my body was exposed to the warm air in the bathing room, and his eyes roved appreciatively over my form. A scowl formed when he saw the blood streaking my thighs.

"I have hurt you," Jacob said as he took a step back.

I followed him, touching his chest, before he could run away. "No, my husband. That is only my maidenhead."

"You were a virgin?" Jacob asked.

I took a step back as if slapped by his words. "Of course, your Grace. I may not have much to my name, but my virtue always remained my own."

He followed me, reaching out his hand, but not touching me. "I did not mean to imply anything, Daisy. Please accept my apology. I was merely taken by surprise."

I nodded, and we both stood naked in silence in the bathing room. I wrapped my arms around myself when a chill washed over me.

"I apologize," Jacob repeated. "Let us not waste the warm water."

I nodded, stepping into the tub closest to me. Closing my eyes, I sighed when the hot water enveloped me and loosened my aching muscles.

"May I?" he asked.

When I opened my eyes, I saw him crouched next to the tub, a washcloth wrapped around his claws.

"You may," I said with a nod.

Jacob picked up my arm and gently slid the washing cloth over my skin. His movements were slow and careful, still so afraid to hurt me. His claws were massive, sharp, and frightening, but padded with the fabric so he could touch me with them in a way that did me no harm.

"How are you feeling?" Jacob asked, his eyes focused on my soft skin. "I was not too..."

"I am feeling wonderful. Breaking my maidenhead hurt for a moment, but that was all my doing. You have given me so much pleasure, my husband. I must thank you for that."

His eyes focused on me again. "I must thank you for allowing me inside of your body. It was the greatest gift you could ever give me."

"I hope to give you that gift, again and again, throughout our marriage."

"It would be my honor," Jacob said.

"Will you not join me in the water?" I asked.

He shook his head as he picked up my other arm. "I prefer to shower in the rain. I have no need for a bath like you do since I do not sweat."

Jacob cleaned the rest of my upper body with gentle movements, never staying in one place too long. When he finished cleaning the parts of me he could reach, he sat back. He dipped the cloth in the water of the empty bath behind him and cleaned off his cock.

I watched him caress his cock, amazed at how it had fit inside of me. It had a slightly darker color than his skin and was long and beautiful. I had always been an admirer of art, and I could confidently say that his cock was a work of art. Every ridge and every vein seemed to have been created out of a need for perfection. It hardened and grew even larger under my eyes.

"It does seem you have left your mark on me," Jacob said.

"How so?" I asked, my eyes still glued to his cock.

"My cock still smells like your desire even when I wash it off," he said. His hand traveled over his chest. "Your hands have left an impression on my skin that even a chisel cannot erase." As he touched his lips, his voice grew huskies. "And your mouth will forever haunt my dreams."

I stretched out my hand, caressing his cold, hard skin. "I intend to leave so many more, my husband," I said.

I leaned over, arching my head up to him, and he took the silent invitation. His lips fit on mine perfectly, as if we were made for each other. I loved his lips on mine, and his taste filling my senses. When we kissed, I felt like I could forget the world around me and the circumstances of how we met. We were just two people, husband, and wife, discovering each other slowly, body, mind, and soul.

The Honeymoon

We fell into a comfortable routine after our delayed wedding night. I woke up before the sun would set, handled the household, and instructed the staff for the night and day to come. After the sunset, he would wake up and we would work together in his study.

Jacob gave me access to all of his books and study material and I consumed the knowledge as if it fed me. Often times I would instigate a sexual encounter, which he would happily accept.

I sat in the chaise close to him one day, engrossed in my reading when he asked me. "I am curious, my wife."

"Tell me," I said as I put my book down to look at him.

"What did you want to ask me the day we met that was so inappropriate?"

A laugh bubbled up inside me as I could feel my cheeks heat up. "It was a silly question."

"I wish to know," Jacob said as a smile grazed his lips.

"I wanted to ask you how old you are. I read somewhere that Gargoyles can live up to hundreds of years."

"Ah, I understand. It is true that we live longer than humans. I am one hundred and fifty years old. I believe we usually live up to around two hundred years."

"You do not look a hundred and fifty years," I said, looking at his stone face, unmarked by age.

I would have estimated him maybe a handful of years older than me at most.

"How could you die?" I asked, imagining his skin impenetrable.

Jacob shrugged, looking away. "There are a few ways a Gargoyle can meet their end in an untimely matter, but when we have lived the life we have needed to live, we simply remain stone. My mother remained asleep after my father..."

Grabbing his hand, I squeezed it comfortingly. "I am sorry. I did not wish to bring up old memories."

"No, it is good for me to share them and for you to know who you married. If I were to lose you, I would not want to continue in this world, as did my mother."

My heart ached at his words. I didn't know how or when it had happened, but our feelings had grown stronger with each passing day, although neither of us had expressed it.

"I understand. But we still have so much time ahead of us. We must enjoy every day we have together, and I think I know the best way to do that," I said as I crawled on his lap.

A smile grazed his lips, and the sadness dissipated from his eyes. I wished to see him happy, but I knew that sharing sorrows helped to elevate the pain.

"How would my wife like to enjoy her time with me today?" Jacob asked.

I was already unbuttoning his pants, craving his cock. It seemed that the more I had of him, the more I needed. As if he was some sort of drug that I craved to feel complete. I had asked my sisters about it, and they had laughed, telling me it was love.

"I would enjoy your cock inside of me," I said.

Before I could pull my skirts aside and sink down on him, he lifted me up and laid me on the desk. With a gasp, I grabbed my skirts as he opened my legs wide, exposing my pussy to the hot air of his study.

"Would you enjoy my tongue as well?" Jacob asked.

"Oh, I believe I would," I said.

"Good," he rumbled as he descended between my legs.

His hands grabbed my legs, keeping them spread wide as his mouth made contact with my pussy. He had become less afraid to hurt me, learning how to position his claws so as not to scratch my skin. The first lick was a long, slow drag from my entrance to my pleasure bud. His tongue was cold and wet on my hot pussy, an exquisite temperature difference that sparked pleasure deep inside of me.

"I crave your taste and your scent on my lips," Jacob growled.

"I crave your tongue and your cock," I moaned.

I watched as his tongue came out again to lick my pussy. It was a darker shade of purple, in stark contrast to my pink pussy. He licked me, again and again, until I was a moaning mess, ready to burst. He dipped his tongue inside of me, stroking me with his cool appendage like he would his cock. Pleasure rose inside of me with each flick, lick, and dip of his tongue. Nothing could compare to how good it felt.

I was moving my hips, trying to get away from him and closer at the same time. His hands tightened around my legs, holding me steady as he pushed his tongue inside of me again. He slowly fucked me with his tongue, sparking pleasure with each thrust, but I needed more to reach my climax.

"Please," I moaned, unable to voice what I needed, but he seemed to understand.

He pulled his tongue back, licking his lips in an obscene manner that made my insides clench. "Does my wife wish to come on my tongue?" Jacob asked.

"Yes, please, Jacob."

"I aim to please," he said before diving back in.

He focused on my pleasure bud, kissing and licking it. His lips and tongue played together to give me pleasure in a way that made everything around me disappear. My moans grew louder and more frequent as pleasure rose inside of me.

His lips closed around my pleasure bud and when he sucked gently on it, it became too much. I burst into a million pieces as pleasure washed over me. My back arched off the desk as my pussy clenched around nothing. Jacob murmured happily against my pussy, lapping up my juices as waves of pleasure flowed through me. His gentle tongue made me come down from my high, but I craved more.

"Fuck me," I moaned as I stretched out my arms to him. "I need my husband. I need your cock."

My Gargoyle stood up, stretching his wings until they reached the bookcases framing us. He was absolutely magnificent, and all mine. Somehow, I could not imagine my life without him. Even though we had only been married for a handful of weeks, I felt a bond with him that only grew stronger with each passing day.

He pulled his pants down, stepping in between my legs. My hands wandered over his chest, loving the smooth, cool texture underneath my palms. His wings shivered as he covered my hands with his.

"I crave your touch," Jacob said. "I do not think I can go a day without your hands on me."

"I do not wish to go a day without touching you," I said with a smile. "Now fill me with your cock, my husband."

"As you wish," Jacob said, grabbing his hard cock, stroking it a few times to coat it in his precum before he positioned it at my opening.

My pussy was wet and sensitive from my recent orgasm, and he slid in easily. His cock stretched me to fit inside. After the pain of the first time, I had only experienced pleasure with him. His cock gave me a deep kind of pleasure only he could give me. He pushed inside of me, stretching me until it burned in the best way as his coolness eased the burn at the same time.

The sounds he made only enhanced my own pleasure of our joining. His face contorted in pleasure as he grunted when he fucked me.

"I love your heat surrounding me," Jacob groaned with eyes closed.

My pussy squeezed around his cock with his husky words, sparking pleasure. I could only imagine how hot I felt against his cold skin.

"Yes, squeeze me tight," Jacob groaned.

I clamped my pussy around him again, earning another strangled groan from him. He moved his hips at a fast pace, fucking me on the desk while I grasped his shoulders to prevent being pushed off. Papers rustled around me, and a book fell on the ground, but we didn't care. We only had eyes for each other, chasing each other high at the same time. He increased his pace as my pussy trembled around his cock, so close to another climax already.

"Take your pleasure," Jacob said, as his eyes focused on me. "I want to see and feel you come around my cock before I spend inside of you."

I let one hand slide in between us, feeling his cock piston in and out of my pussy. I found my pleasure bud throbbing and sensitive. It was too much to touch it directly, so I circled around it, teasing it, and increasing my own pleasure. His cold cock did amazing things to my insides as my finger pleasured me from the outside.

"I am so close," I moaned when I could feel my climax rising to the surface.

"Yes, come for me," Jacob groaned as he fucked me harder. "Squeeze my cock with your pleasure."

His words ignited my orgasm, and I screamed out his name in pleasure. My pussy squeezed around his cock as my body trembled with my release. His wings shivered and his body trembled as I saw his face contorted in pleasure. He came, making a wholly sensual sound, a low rumble of pleasure I could feel vibrating through me. His cock throbbed as he filled me with his release. Pleasure washed over me as my pussy milked his cock, craving his seed. I could never get enough of him, only wanting him more the more I had him.

When the last tremors of pleasure left my body, he pulled out of me. His seed leaked from my pussy, and I watched it trickle down my legs onto his desk. He had come inside of me multiple times already, but there were no signs I was with child.

"My sister is pregnant again," I said absentmindedly.

"Which one?" Jacob asked as he grabbed a cloth to wipe away his seed.

"Both I think," I said. "How do Gargoyles come into existence?" I asked, looking up at him.

His hands froze as his wings shivered. After he took a deep breath, he continued cleaning his seed away.

"Female Gargoyles go in heat once every decade. When they mate with a male Gargoyle, they can produce eggs together."

"Can we..."

I let my question die down as he looked at me and I could already see the answer in his eyes. It made sense thinking about it. I had never heard of a Gargoyle interspecies couple or even seen Gargoyle children. Somehow, I had never imagined myself having children, but the knowledge of its impossibility changed something inside of me. A sense of calmness washed over me.

"I apologize Daisy. I thought you knew," Jacob shook his head, averting his eyes. "I never intended for this marriage to become..."

"Real?" I asked as I sat up and pulled my skirts down.

"No. I mean, yes. I... Daisy. Can I be enough for you to be happy?"

I looked up at him and saw the anguish on his face. I got off the desk and stepped in between his legs, putting my hands on his chest.

"Oh my husband, do not confuse my silence with anger. I was merely gathering my thoughts. Why would you think you are not enough for me? I was a spinster with nothing to my name and you made me a Duchess and shared your knowledge and wealth with me," I said, waving around his study that held more books than I could ever read in a lifetime. "How could you ever think you were not enough? I crave your touch and your mind. I love our shared silence almost as much as I love your cock buried inside of me. My husband, I love you."

Saying those words out loud for the first time made me realize them to be true. I loved my husband, and I knew that we did not need children for that love to keep growing.

"You love me?" Jacob asked, his eyes wide and his wings trembling.

"Yes, you impossible Gargoyle. Why do you think I sleep during the day and come here every night?" I asked with a laugh.

"I just assumed- I do not know."

"Have you ever loved someone?" I asked.

"Many decades ago, I thought I did, but it all pales in comparison to what I feel for you, Daisy. My Duchess, my wife, my love."

"So you love me too?" I asked, somehow needing to hear him say it.

"I do. I love you," Jacob said and kissed me.

The End

Epilogue

A *few months later*
"I received a letter from Violet," I said.

"How is she doing?" Jacob asked, looking up from his desk.

I read it in silence, a smile blooming on my face.

"She had a healthy baby boy and inherited our family's estate. She is inviting us to come visit."

"That is wonderful. We shall arrange for it," he said with a nod, making a note on a paper.

"Thank you, my husband."

"Anything for you, my darling wife," Jacob said as he pulled my chair to him.

"Hmm, anything?" I asked as I crawled on his lap.

I rubbed his cock covered in fabric, and I could feel it hardening underneath my touch. He was always so responsive to my touches, still so grateful for my interest in him.

"My heart, body, and soul belong to you, Daisy."

"Good thing I gave you mine in exchange," I said and kissed him.

His tongue danced with mine as I moaned into the kiss. For a Gargoyle who had been alone for so long, he quickly learned how to please his human wife. I freed his cock from its confinements as I pushed my skirts to the side. I craved his cock inside of me, filling that ache that only he could make disappear. My pussy was already wet for him. He only needed to say a few words, caress my skin, or kiss me, and I was ready for him.

With a moan, I let myself sink down on his cock. He stretched me to my limit, but it was a pleasurable burn, soothed by his cool skin, only he could give me. The sounds he made and the way his face contorted in pleasure were everything that made my heart soar with love.

"I love you," I moaned as I started to move.

"And I love you, my wonderful wife."

His hands grabbed my hips through the fabric as he helped me bounce on his cock. Slowly but surely, he became less afraid to hurt me with his claws, learning how to position or cover them so as to not harm my delicate skin. I loved his hands on me, aiding me to reach our combined pleasure.

Pleasure rose inside of me with every thrust of his cock, but I always needed more to reach my climax. I let my hand slip in between us, locating my pleasure bud, circling it in slow movements.

"Beautiful," Jacob growled as he looked at my face, contorted in pleasure. "You are marvelous as you take your pleasure."

My pussy squeezed around his cock, loving his rough words, encouraging me to reach my high. Every moment with him filled me with happiness and pleasure. Even doing mundane tasks together filled my heart with joy.

"I want your pleasure as well, my husband," I moaned.

"You give me so much pleasure," Jacob moaned as my pussy squeezed around his cock again.

He increased his pace, fucking me hard until I was a moaning mess filled with pleasure. Each thrust ignited something inside of me, his cock filling me in a way that made me feel whole and complete. Our sound of pleasure filled the library, making it a room of lust and connection.

After a few more thrusts, I could feel his cock throb inside of me as my pussy trembled. Another flick of my finger and pleasure washed over me. Wave after wave of pleasure filled me as my body shivered and his wings spread wide. His cock throbbed and filled me with his seed as his beautiful face contorted with pleasure.

I loved coming together with him, feeling so close we could almost be one. My Gargoyle husband, mine in every sense of the word.

The End

Bonus Epilogue

Many years later

"Welcome," I said as I hugged my youngest sister, Daisy.

Lilly already arrived with her husband and children, who were playing outside in the warm summer weather with mine. It was great to be in my family home raising my own family, but it was even better having my sisters here with me.

The men went out to hunt, and my nanny entertained the children so me and my sisters could catch up. So much has happened over the past years, and even though we exchanged many letters, it was great to see them again.

"It is good to be together again," Lilly said, putting her hands on mine and Daisy's.

I patted it with a smile, glad to see both of them content and married.

"It is," Daisy replied with a nod.

She had grown into such a beautiful woman, and became a Duchess all on her own, but still did not have any children to speak of.

"So how are you and the Duke fairing? Any exciting news on the way?" I asked, trying to be subtle but failing miserably.

Daisy smirked and nodded. "We have indeed some exciting news."

I held my breath as she sat up a bit straighter and looked at me. "We are going to Greece next month," she said.

"Oh. That is lovely," I said.

Daisy squeezed my hand and smiled. "I know what you want me to say, but it is not in the cards for us, my dear sister, and I am content with our marriage as it is. We have a world to see, knowledge to consume, and time to spend together. I never wanted to be a mother like you two did."

"I know, but-"

Before I could say anything I would probably regret, Lilly interjected. "We do have exciting news to share," she said as she caressed her stomach. "It seems as though my husband is intent on filling all the rooms of our house."

"Oh, so joyous news, my sister," I said as I focused on her.

Lilly's eyes turned dreamy as she looked over the garden. "He never misses an opportunity to put me on a flat surface and ravage me."

I gasped as Daisy snorted. "I will assure my husband does not lack in that department. If it were up to him, we would spend all night in his office, and never even go out."

Even though their words shocked me, both my sisters had grown up into beautiful women in joyful marriages and even though they differed from mine, I knew they were happy.

As the sun set, and the children went to sleep, the Duke arrived with the whoosh of his wings. He landed next to Daisy, surrounding her with his grand, purple wings, pulling back several moments later, leaving my sister a little more breathless and her lips a touch darker.

My husband and the Earl returned from the hunt, laughing and talking together, but as soon as the massive Minotaur set eyes on his wife, he pulled Lilly into a hug, kissing her in a way that was fully improper in company.

I diverted my eyes, focusing on my own love. The big green Orc cupped my cheek and kissed me gently.

"How was the afternoon tea?" Grant asked.

"Good. They seem happy," I said.

"They do. And are you still happy with your lowly Orc stable hand?"

"You know you are Lord of this land now," I said as I played with the top button of his shirt he always left open.

Grant still only wore comfortable clothing, even though he had a title to match my brothers-in-law. Since he spent more time on the land or in the stables than he did in the old office of my father, I didn't mind.

"As long as I am Lord of your pussy, I am happy," Grant growled as he pulled me against his body.

I could feel his hardness poke my soft stomach, and arousal coursed through me, but this was not the time nor the place to let those feelings bloom.

"We have guests," I hissed as I looked into his gorgeous brown eyes, burning with desire for me.

Even though I wasn't the young, slender woman he had married so many years ago, my Orc still desired me as much as that first night together.

"They seem preoccupied," Grant murmured in my ear as he let his tongue glide over the shell of it, making pleasurable shivers wash over my body.

I looked over and saw both my sisters in matching positions with their husbands. I didn't need to worry about their happiness as I saw the love radiate from them both. We all found our perfect match and loving husband in vastly different ways, and I was happy for them.

THE END

Authors Note

I love these sisters and their monster husbands so much that it hurts to say goodbye to them! I hope the little bonus Epilogue helped ease the pain of letting them go.

Every single sister got their happy ending that worked out for them in their own way.

Violet has a family with Grant and lives in her family home. Lilly and Ian keep on adding to their family until all the rooms in their house are filled and Daisy and Jacob are off the see the world together

Anyway, I hope you enjoyed this historical monster erotica collection! Please leave a rating and/or a review if you did.

About the author

Lilith Leana writes what she loves; Monster, fantasy, and sci-fi erotica.

Born and raised in Belgium, she devours ebooks as if it heals her. In her day job she loves to organize, plan and make schedules for other people, but when the night falls she can let loose with her fantasies which star all kinds of Monsters and Human couplings.

YOU CAN ALSO FIND ME on:

New Author Website: https://lilithleana.wordpress.com

New Newsletter! Sign Up to be kept up to date about my new releases, sales, character art, and giveaways: Sign Up Form[1]

Instagram: https://www.instagram.com/lilithleana

Etsy Shop: https://www.etsy.com/be/shop/SteamyPublishing

Or you can email me: lilith.leana666@gmail.com

DEAR READER

If you enjoyed this book, please consider leaving a review. Indie writers depend on reviews to keep writing and publishing.

Thank you so much ❤

Lilith

---

1.   https://dashboard.mailerlite.com/forms/533589/95138330138642151/share

Also by the author

Series & Collections

<u>Creature Loving Volume 1: A Monster Erotica Collection</u>[1]
<u>Creature Loving Volume 2: A Monster Erotica Collection</u>[2]
<u>Creature Loving Volume 3: A Monster Erotica Collection</u>[3]
<u>Creature Loving Volume 4: A Monster Erotica Collection</u>[4]
<u>Creature Loving Volume 5: A Monster Erotica Collection</u>[5]
<u>Creature Loving Holidays 1: A Monster Erotica Collection</u>[6]
<u>Grim Lovers 1: An Erotic Fairytale Collection</u>[7]
<u>Grim Lovers 2: An Erotic Fairytale Collection</u>[8]
<u>Grim Lovers 3: An Erotic Fairytale Collection</u>[9]
<u>My Ghostly Lover</u>[10]
<u>My Orc Mate</u>[11]

---

1. https://books2read.com/u/47gLkj

2. https://books2read.com/u/47VMwA

3. https://books2read.com/u/bW0pk1

4. https://books2read.com/u/3LxQD1

5. https://books2read.com/u/4AaD90

6. https://books2read.com/u/bp6Yyg

7. https://books2read.com/u/4AA7Zp

8. https://books2read.com/u/mZpjNe

9. https://books2read.com/u/3J5B2J

10. https://books2read.com/u/3J6dxJ

11. https://books2read.com/u/3yd90L

Brief summaries of other Monster Erotica titles by Lilith Leana

Bathing with the Akkorokamui[1]

Ava's trip to Japan ends in the beautiful village, Kurokawa Onsen, famous for its hot springs. She gets the most pleasurable and relaxing surprise when she enters the lair of the Akkorokamui.

Akkorokamui lives to heal people with the use of its tentacles. Ava has tension everywhere in her body, and it will do its utmost best to let her unwind in the most satisfying way possible.

ON A DATE WITH THE Yeti[2]

Willa has a crush on a cute, shy Yeti. When he asks her out for a date, she immediately says yes, not realizing that a date with a Yeti is much more than just dining together.

Cole the Yeti has finally mustered up the courage to ask out the human from the shop he visits weekly. Will she become his mate and let him fill her with Yeti babies?

COOKING WITH THE TROLL[3]

Amy wants to save her farm by working together with a famous Troll Chef. She didn't expect his hands and ability to create the most amazing flavors with the simplest of ingredients to impress her so much.

1. https://books2read.com/u/3LVqEX

2. https://books2read.com/u/4jYqrD

3. https://books2read.com/u/ml6kE9

Ragnok likes to be alone in his mountain cabin surrounded by pure ingredients to cook with, but when Amy barges in his space, he cannot let her go without having a taste of her first.

NESTING WITH THE SHIFTER[4]

Vanya is an Omega Wolf shifter who suddenly feels the need to nest. In a remote mountain cabin, she carefully arranges her nest, preparing for her fated Mate's arrival.

Kai is a Mountain Lion shifter passing through when he smells his Mate. He wants to help her build her nest and fill it with pups and cubs.

CHASED BY THE GARGOYLE[5]

With a mix of anticipation and uncertainty, Sadie arrives at her first monthly Human-Monster mixer. Little does she know, her evening is about to take an unexpected turn when a captivating Gargoyle sets his sights on her, his intentions extending far beyond just a chase.

As Sadie heads to the Human-Monster Mixer, William sees it as the ideal moment to finally reveal his interest in her, after secretly watching her for a while. The moment he tastes her, he realizes he can't let her slip away from his grasp.

---

4. https://books2read.com/u/4jYkBl

5. https://books2read.com/u/brMd8k

www.ingramcontent.com/pod-product-compliance
Lightning Source LLC
Chambersburg PA
CBHW031447130726

47989CB00003B/1302